"What brings you to the Rose City?" Brett asked.

Laurel concentrated on his eyes. Eyes that belied the strength in his jaw and ruggedness of his nose. Brett Matthews looked as if he would be more comfortable hiking in the mountains than making millions in the stock market. "I—I came to see you."

"Really? After all these months? It's been, what? Almost four months since the annulment? All that time without a word," Brett said.

Laurel stared at the carpet. This wasn't going the way she'd planned. She wanted to tell him the truth, but pride wouldn't let her admit what had happened—that she was now responsible not only for herself, but... She met his eyes. "Several family matters came up that required my full attention."

Brett's gaze seemed to bore straight into her soul, and she swallowed hard.

"So," he said, "which are you going to tell me about first? Being broke or being pregnant?"

Dear Reader,

There's something for *everyone* in a Silhouette Romance, be it moms (or daughters!) or women who've found—or who still seek!—that special man in their lives. Just revel in this month's diverse offerings as we continue to celebrate Silhouette's 20th Anniversary.

It's last stop: STORKVILLE, USA, as Karen Rose Smith winds this adorable series to its dramatic conclusion. A virgin with amnesia finds shelter in the town sheriff's home, but will she find lasting love with *Her Honor-Bound Lawman*? *New York Times* bestselling author Kasey Michaels brings her delightful trilogy THE CHANDLERS REQUEST… to an end with the sparkling bachelor-auction story *Raffling Ryan*. *The Millionaire's Waitress Wife* becomes the latest of THE BRUBAKER BRIDES as Carolyn Zane's much-loved miniseries continues.

In the second installment of Donna Clayton's SINGLE DOCTOR DADS, *The Doctor's Medicine Woman* holds the key to his adoption of twin Native American boys—and to his guarded heart. *The Third Kiss* is a charmer from Leanna Wilson—a must-read pretend engagement story! And a one-night marriage that began with "The Wedding March" leads to *The Wedding Lullaby* in Melissa McClone's latest offering.…

Next month, return to Romance for more of THE BRUBAKER BRIDES and SINGLE DOCTOR DADS, as well as the newest title in Sandra Steffen's BACHELOR GULCH series!

Happy Reading!

Mary-Theresa Hussey

Mary-Theresa Hussey
Senior Editor

Please address questions and book requests to:
Silhouette Reader Service
U.S.: 3010 Walden Ave., P.O. Box 1325, Buffalo, NY 14269
Canadian: P.O. Box 609, Fort Erie, Ont. L2A 5X3

The Wedding Lullaby

MELISSA McCLONE

SILHOUETTE *Romance*

Published by Silhouette Books

America's Publisher of Contemporary Romance

To Annelise Robey
for her help, support and encouragement
and
to my husband, Tom,
for all that he does each and every day.

SILHOUETTE BOOKS

ISBN 0-373-19485-4

THE WEDDING LULLABY

Visit Silhouette at www.eHarlequin.com

Printed in U.S.A.

Books by Melissa McClone

Silhouette Romance

If the Ring Fits... #1431
The Wedding Lullaby #1485

Silhouette Yours Truly

Fiancé for the Night

MELISSA McCLONE

With a degree in mechanical engineering from Stanford University, the last thing Melissa McClone ever thought she would be doing is writing romance novels, but analyzing engines for a major U.S. airline just couldn't compete with her "happily-ever-afters."

When she isn't writing, caring for her toddler and newborn or doing laundry, Melissa loves to curl up on the couch with a cup of tea, her cats and a good book. She is also a big fan of *The X-Files* and enjoys watching home decorating shows to get ideas for her house—a 1939 cottage that is *slowly* being renovated.

Melissa lives in Lake Oswego, Oregon, with her own real-life hero husband, daughter, son, two lovable but oh-so-spoiled indoor cats and a no-longer-stray outdoor kitty who decided to call the garage home. Melissa loves to hear from readers. You can write to her at P.O. Box 63, Lake Oswego, OR 97034.

IT'S OUR 20th ANNIVERSARY!
We'll be celebrating all year,
Continuing with these fabulous titles,
On sale in November 2000.

Desire

#1327 Marriage Prey
Annette Broadrick

#1328 Her Perfect Man
Mary Lynn Baxter

#1329 A Cowboy's Gift
Anne McAllister

#1330 Husband—or Enemy?
Caroline Cross

#1331 The Virgin and the Vengeful Groom
Dixie Browning

#1332 Night Wind's Woman
Sheri WhiteFeather

Romance

#1480 Her Honor-Bound Lawman
Karen Rose Smith

#1481 Raffling Ryan
Kasey Michaels

#1482 The Millionaire's Waitress Wife
Carolyn Zane

#1483 The Doctor's Medicine Woman
Donna Clayton

#1484 The Third Kiss
Leanna Wilson

#1485 The Wedding Lullaby
Melissa McClone

Special Edition

#1357 A Man Alone
Lindsay McKenna

#1358 The Rancher Next Door
Susan Mallery

#1359 Sophie's Scandal
Penny Richards

#1360 The Bridal Quest
Jennifer Mikels

#1361 Baby of Convenience
Diana Whitney

#1362 Just Eight Months Old...
Tori Carrington

Intimate Moments

#1039 The Brands Who Came for Christmas
Maggie Shayne

#1040 Hero at Large
Robyn Amos

#1041 Made for Each Other
Doreen Owens Malek

#1042 Hero for Hire
Marie Ferrarella

#1043 Dangerous Liaisons
Maggie Price

#1044 Dad in Blue
Shelley Cooper

Prologue

"Talk about a lucky roll of the dice." Henry Davenport's canary-eating smile said it all. "I do believe I've outdone myself this year."

"You have." Brett Matthews grinned at his best man, standing next to him at the front of the Love Dove Wedding Nest, a cheesy hole-in-the-wall chapel in Reno, Nevada. "But no one would have expected any less."

Henry was the epitome of idle rich, a trust fund baby with nothing better to do with his time than watch his inheritance grow. Every year, a group of Henry's friends and acquaintances met for a Bacchanalian celebration on his birthday, April Fools' Day, and two of the party goers partook in an "adventure" dreamed up by their host extraordinaire.

This year, the birthday boy wanted to throw the tackiest wedding of the year. A roll of the dice had selected the bride and groom. Brett had rolled a pair of sixes. His intended, the same. Now all they had to say was "I do."

Henry had provided everything from the wedding apparel and the ice-cube-size, garish wedding ring to the high-priced, highly qualified lawyer who had drawn up a heavy as a paperweight prenuptial agreement to protect the vast family fortunes of the parties involved and oversee the annulment proceedings.

Not that Brett's vast wealth came from family money, as everyone else's did. It was new money with that fresh-from-the-mint scent. But for once that didn't seem to matter to anyone.

Henry jabbed Brett. "It's not too late to bow out."

A ten thousand dollar penalty fee to one of Henry's favorite charities allowed guests to say no to participating in an adventure. "That wouldn't be in the spirit of the celebration."

Henry's smile widened. "You've come a long way, Matthews."

Brett had. His entire life he'd wanted to show the "old money" kids he'd grown up with that he was more than the Davenports' housekeeper's bastard son. Thanks to Henry's invitation this year, Brett was getting the chance. He knew he should be past the niggling sense of insecurity, but despite everything he had achieved in his life, this was the acceptance he needed most.

He was about to marry the society princess herself, Laurel Worthington, a fun-loving blueblood who graced the Chicago society columns and pages of *Town and Country* on a regular basis.

He'd only met Laurel this afternoon, but she was perfect, exactly the kind of woman he would want for a wife—beautiful, refined and connected. Maybe he could convince his bride to start dating him. Maybe he could convince her not to annul the marriage. Maybe...

The sequined-clad Elvis impersonator minister tapped him on the shoulder. "Ready?"

Brett nodded.

The minister played "Love Me Tender" on his guitar. Cynthia Sterling, maid of honor and friend of the bride, sauntered down the aisle. The full skirt of her stick-of-bubblegum-pink satin bridesmaid dress swayed, and the crinolines underneath rustled.

"Last chance to jilt your bride," Henry whispered.

Brett ignored him. Ignored the pounding of his heart. Ignored the sweat dampening his collar.

This was it. This was really it.

He stared at his bride and sucked in a breath. Laurel Worthington should have looked ridiculous wearing the garage sale reject bridal apparel and carrying a bouquet of silk carnations that had seen better days.

But she didn't. He'd never seen a more stunning bride. She was the kind of woman he dreamed about dating, loving, marrying. Talk about icing on the cake. He grinned.

She flashed him a shy smile, and his heart melted.

Out of your league, Matthews.

Not any longer, he reminded himself.

With slow steps, she followed the path worn into the carpeted aisle. Her polyester lace gown hugged each and every one of her luscious curves. Her light brown hair shimmered beneath a rhinestone tiara with a ten-inch puff of tulle veil.

When she reached the altar, she extended her arm to Brett. Her sparkling blue eyes met his, and he wanted to forget this was all an act. He swallowed the lump lodged in his throat and took her hand in his. So delicate, so soft, so lovely. And his…at least for tonight. Smiling, he faced the minister.

Thanks to a roll of the dice, Brett Matthews had made it. He finally belonged.

Chapter One

She'd made it. Over two thousand miles. And on her own.

Laurel smiled, one of the few real, teeth-baring smiles that had graced her lips in nearly four months. If she didn't already feel dizzy from the exhaust fumes of the Tri-met bus pulling away from the curb, she would spin around and celebrate.

Making the trip west and arriving in one piece was a huge accomplishment. A success she should be proud of. If only there hadn't been so many failures…

A mist of cool raindrops wet her face, and she quickly wiped the water away. She refused to let anyone think she'd been crying. Her days of tears and feeling sorry for herself were over. She had too much to do, too little time to wallow in self-pity.

Raising her chin, Laurel took a step toward the building in front of her. Somewhere inside the cement and glass fortress was Brett Matthews.

Brett.

The thought of his name made Laurel's stomach do not only a cartwheel, but a back flip, too. Not an easy feat considering the circumstances, but the sight of the building where he worked was more than enough to make her anxious and a little nauseous.

Nickel-size raindrops fell from the darkening sky and splattered on the cement. So much for a light afternoon shower, but Oregon was known for its rain. A few more minutes of this and she'd be soaked to the skin. Time to get inside. She couldn't afford to catch a cold or worse.

She adjusted the bag on her shoulder and rolled her suitcase along the slick pavement, careful to keep it steady. Everything she owned, everything left from a life that no longer existed, was contained in the two bags.

But Laurel wouldn't look back. From now on, she was only looking forward. All she wanted was to make a fresh start. All she needed was the chance.

She stepped inside the high-rise, brushed the water from her knee-length raincoat and glanced at the building directory. She spotted Brett's company, Matthews Global Investments. Full of purpose and resolve, she hurried to the elevator.

As the floors whizzed by, she combed her fingers through her wet hair and tried not to think about how desperately it needed a cut—something she hadn't had in months.

She removed her coat and smoothed the wrinkles from her blouse. Not much she could do about the soiled hem of her pants and her scuffed shoes. No doubt she looked like something the cat dragged in.

The only thing intact were her nails. Her mother would be proud that Laurel hadn't bitten them to the quick. Instead, she'd spent the long bus ride filing them to perfection in between restless naps and daydreams. Not exactly a professional manicure, but her weekly visits to the salon were over.

Ding. The elevator doors opened at her destination—the twelfth floor. As she stepped out, she found herself in a lobby, staring at the words *Matthews Global Investments* displayed in brass lettering on the wall behind a reception desk.

"Welcome to MGI." The smartly dressed receptionist smiled. "May I help you?"

No time to prepare herself. No time for a calming breath. No time to turn around. Laurel hesitated, but only for a moment. "I'm here to see Brett—I mean, Mr. Matthews."

"Your name?" the receptionist asked.

"Laurel Worthington."

The woman scanned a sheet of paper attached to a clipboard, then looked up. "Do you have an appointment?"

"No."

"May I ask what this is pertaining to?"

Laurel swallowed hard. "I, uh…"

As the receptionist waited expectantly, Laurel felt lightheaded under the scrutiny, and a kernel of panic lodged in her chest. She had to say something to guarantee she would be allowed to see Brett. She *had* to see him. "I'm his wife."

The receptionist looked stunned. "His wife?"

Oh, no. Had Laurel really said that? Heat rushed to her cheeks. "Ex-wife, actually."

The receptionist adjusted her headset and snapped her jaw closed. She pushed a button on her phone. "Debbie, Mr. Matthews's ex-wife is here."

Visibly interested, the receptionist stared at her and smiled. She waited for what seemed an eternity before speaking again. "I'll send her back."

Yes. Brett was going to see her. Excited, Laurel balled her hands. Now, to remain calm. Stick to her plan. Say what she'd come to say.

"Go through the double doors. His assistant, Debbie, will show you to his office. You may leave your luggage here."

Laurel smiled. "Thank you."

As she stepped toward the doors, she tried to regain her composure. The brass doorknob felt cold beneath her palm. Holding on to it a moment longer than necessary, she let the coolness chase away her embarrassed heat. *Ready or not.* Laurel opened the door.

"Hi." A perky blonde wearing a navy dress with matching pumps greeted her. Except for her multiple-pierced ears, she was dressed for success. "I'm Debbie Taylor, Brett's assistant. I don't mean to be personal, but are you really his ex-wife?"

"Uh, yes." Laurel caught a whiff of Debbie's jasmine scented perfume and wondered how personal Brett was with his charming assistant. Not that it was any of her business. "I'm Laurel Worthington."

"Nice to meet you." Debbie smiled. "He never told us he'd been married."

Laurel wasn't surprised. Men had a way of forgetting her. Just look at her ex-fiancé, Charles Kingsley. "Our marriage was..." a joke, a game, an adventure "...brief."

Debbie led her down a hallway past several other doors and conference rooms. Everything about the decor of MGI was stunning. It was exactly what Laurel expected of Brett. All of the plants were green and thriving, the oil paintings and their gilt frames perfectly aligned. From the thick, hunter-green carpet to the gleaming cherry desks, the subdued elegance and rich atmosphere left no doubt about the success of the company, nor its business—making money for its wealthy clients. She envied Brett, envied the way he'd made something as successful as MGI on his own.

She saw another office, with Brett's name on the mahogany door. Laurel inhaled sharply. She wanted to touch the letters and imagine that her own name was engraved there.

"Please make yourself comfortable. Brett's in a meeting and will be with you shortly," Debbie explained, showing her in. "Can I get you something to drink? A cup of coffee or a soda?"

"No, thank you."

"If there's anything you need, just let me know." Debbie closed the door.

I need my life back. I need my head examined. I need Brett. Laurel repressed a sigh, sat on a leather wingback chair and tapped her toes. She glanced at the door, willing it to open. She wanted to get this over with.

How long would his meeting last? She stared at his desk and did a double take.

Brett's office surprised her. Not the decor, but the order. Everything on his desk was in its perfect place, from the files and newspapers to his pencils and pens. Not one sheet of paper out of alignment, not one rubber band. She didn't even see any yellow Post-It notes anywhere. She would never have expected Brett to be so neat and tidy.

Not when he'd left a trail of his clothes strewn on the floor as he'd made his way to her. Not when he'd skillfully removed her wedding gown and not-so-gracefully chucked it across the hotel room. Not when the bathroom looked as if a tornado had ripped through it after a Jacuzzi for two.

But it had only been one night.

One short, but oh-so-glorious night.

If only it had been real...

Upon waking, she'd quickly realized she'd mistaken the warmth and security of his arms for something more than a stolen moment. Given her situation, it had been easy to do, but that didn't change the facts. He was a complete stranger.

So what if he'd been tender, generous and giving? So what if he'd made her feel safe, cherished, even loved? So what if she still saw his smile when she closed her eyes at night? She couldn't forget that those things meant nothing in the light of day. What they had shared had been nothing more than a fantasy.

No matter how much she might want to believe in romance and love at first sight, she knew love could not exist between two people whose only common bond was a few hours spent in bed together.

Even if those hours had been the most incredible of her entire life.

But what she had to do now had nothing to do with make-believe love or amazing sex or the magical night spent in Brett's arms. It had to do with the future. Brett Matthews might be a stranger, but he was the only one who could help her.

Seconds passed like hours, and she rubbed her belly. She wished she'd brought something to eat and could grab a nap for a few minutes. But this wasn't the time to be hungry or tired. She had to be strong.

The door finally opened. ''Laurel?''

The sound of Brett's voice sent a shiver of pleasure down her spine. Although they had known one another for only a short time, a familiar—comforting—feeling washed over her. He stepped inside his office and closed the door.

The sight of him made her head spin and her mouth go

dry. The ends of his dark brown hair curled slightly and brushed his collar, and made her want to twirl her fingers through his hair one more time.

He wore navy slacks, a white, long-sleeved dress shirt and a tie with endangered animals on it. She'd seen him in a tuxedo; she'd seen him naked. Laurel struggled to put this new image of Brett Matthews, successful financial advisor and author, into perspective.

He was more attractive than she remembered. Maybe not movie-star gorgeous, but he was handsome and one hundred percent male.

For a split second, she wanted to throw her arms around him and ask him to make everything okay. But she knew better. Laurel might need his help, but she was the only one she could rely on.

"Hi." It was the only word she could manage.

He frowned. "Did you have to tell them you were my ex-wife?"

No "hello," no "how have you been," no "I've been thinking about you." Not even a smile or a hint of a grin. "It slipped out. I was afraid they wouldn't let me see you."

"I'm going to have a helluva time explaining this."

"Sorry."

He studied her. "I thought you'd be with Henry and the gang, touring the vineyards of Bordeaux."

The gang wasn't her gang any longer, and she'd lost track of most of them and their travels in the last few months. Friendship only went so far in certain circles. "I, um, decided to pass."

"Maybe next year, then."

She shrugged, even though she knew that next year she'd be lucky if she could afford a bottle of red table wine. "You never know."

"No, you don't."

Brett leaned against his desk and raised an eyebrow, bringing attention to a small scar above his left brow. It gave him a dangerous, bad-boy look. Maybe that's why she'd found him so…appealing in Reno. A bad boy on the outside, a teddy bear on the inside.

"What brings you to the Rose City?" he asked.

She'd rehearsed this moment a million times. Laurel took a deep breath and concentrated on his milk-chocolate eyes. Eyes that belied the strength in his jaw and ruggedness of his nose. A nose that must have been broken at least once. Truth be told, he looked as if he would be more comfortable hiking in the mountains or riding on the back of a horse than making millions in the stock market and telling others how to do the same. "I—I came to see you."

"Really? After all these months?"

Laurel nodded.

"I'm surprised. It's been, what? Almost four months since Reno? All that time without a word—no e-mail, phone call, letter."

"Those things work two ways. Besides, we never said we'd keep in touch."

"Yes, they do, and no, we didn't."

"I planned to, but when I got back to Chicago…" *My life really fell apart. Worse than I could have imagined.* Laurel stared at the carpet. This wasn't going the way she'd planned. She wanted to tell him the truth, that she and her mother had been and still were sinking faster than the *Titanic,* but she couldn't. Pride wouldn't let her admit what had happened, what her own stupidity had allowed to happen. How could Laurel explain that when she'd thought things couldn't get any worse, they had? And she was now responsible not only for herself, but… She met his eyes. "Several family matters came up that required my full attention."

It wasn't the whole truth, but it wasn't a lie, either.

Brett's gaze seemed to bore straight into her soul, and she swallowed hard. Not since their wedding night, when she'd stood before him offering the only thing she had to give—herself—had she felt so vulnerable.

"I'm sorry I didn't contact you sooner," she admitted.

"I'm sure you are." He folded his arms across his chest. "So?"

The accusation she heard in that simple, two letter word made her stiffen, but she hadn't come all this way for nothing. She met his steady gaze. "So, what?"

"So which are you going to tell me about first? Being broke or being pregnant?"

Brett watched Laurel. It took her a full sixty seconds to regain her composure, but her wide, topaz-blue eyes told him he'd caught her off guard. Good. That's what he'd wanted to do after the hell she'd put him through, but the genuine shock on her face took away any pleasure he might have received.

"Y-y-you knew?" she asked. "How?"

His throat constricted as if a noose had tightened around his neck. He'd been feeling this way ever since learning the truth about Laurel Worthington from a private investigator a month ago and having him follow her ever since. "I heard a few rumors, so I checked them out."

"I…I don't understand." She wet her lips. "You knew I was pregnant, but you never tried to get in touch with me, find out if…"

"Is it mine?"

At the flash of hurt in her eyes, Brett knew it was, but he wanted to hear *her* say it.

She brushed a strand of hair behind her ear. "Why didn't you 'check it out' yourself?"

At least she hadn't lost her spunk. The silver-spoon set never did. He was happy to see she still had a spine, however fragile. After what she'd been through... He hardened his heart against the thought.

He couldn't afford to let down his guard, allow emotions to override logic, not even for an instant. Because with Laurel, an instant was all it took. Just an instant of weakness to bring a man to his knees. He'd been that man the night of their honeymoon and had played right into her hands. A hard lesson to learn, but one he wouldn't allow to happen again.

"Is it mine?" he repeated.

"Yes." She looked at him straight on, daring him to contradict her.

A baby. His baby.

Hearing about her pregnancy from a secondary party had been one thing. Having her sit in his office and confirm it was another. He felt as if his head might explode.

As reality sunk in, he tried to summon some sort of protest to keep her from realizing how deeply the truth affected him. His chest tightened, and he found it difficult to breathe.

He was going to be a *father*.

He would get the chance to finally right the wrongs of his own childhood. Give his baby all he'd lacked growing up.

He'd planned what he wanted to do—had been going to see her as soon as the current work crisis had been resolved—but all those plans seemed totally inadequate, totally inappropriate at this moment. His lawyer had warned Brett that Laurel would most likely want him to support her in the manner to which she was accustomed.

Writing her a blank check had seemed like the best way to ensure he was a part of the baby's life. But Brett didn't want to be just a weekend parent. That wasn't good enough for either his child or him.

But before he took steps to remedy that situation, he needed a few answers. "How did this happen?"

"Brett, you know—"

"We used protection."

"Nothing is foolproof."

He gritted his teeth. "Did you want this to happen?"

"I…" She stared at the carpet, then raised her gaze to his. "No, but my world was falling apart. Maybe subconsciously I was looking for a way to keep it all together."

Subconsciously? She couldn't have planned her salvation any better, and he couldn't have been a more willing participant.

Be careful what you wish for….

But in Reno, he hadn't known she wasn't the woman of his dreams. She wasn't wealthy, refined and connected. She was nothing more than a fraud.

"The baby is yours," she insisted. "You're the only one I've ever been with."

Despite her previous engagement, she'd been a virgin on their wedding night, and the P.I. hadn't turned up any lovers since her trip to Reno. "I believe you."

She tilted her chin as if she couldn't care less whether he believed her or not. "I suppose I should thank you for that."

"Don't bother."

"If that's what you want."

Old money through and through. She might not have a penny to her name, but the attitude remained. What a fool he'd been. She'd been so sweet—his blushing bride. Being with her had made him feel as if he belonged, and he hadn't wanted to let go. It had been too easy to imagine their "marriage" to be real, to be permanent.

When they'd reached the hotel room, the pretending should have stopped, but as he'd carried her over the threshold of the honeymoon suite, taking her to bed had seemed like the next logical, the most natural, step to take. He'd assumed she knew what she was getting into. He'd assumed she was anything but a virgin. He'd assumed wrong.

Now she was pregnant.

Broke.

And his responsibility.

He had to give her credit. For someone who'd gone to hell and back, she looked remarkably unchanged. Her wet hair looked more like the color of molasses than the caramel he remembered, but it brought back memories of the heart-shaped hot tub they'd shared. He forced the unwelcome image from his mind.

She didn't look pregnant, but he couldn't tell much with her seated. The changes, if any, were subtle. Her breasts looked fuller and the buttons on her white, wrinkled blouse strained a little. Her black pants fit loosely, but the bottom of her shirt covered her waist and stomach. He wanted to touch her belly to convince himself a baby grew inside.

Anger darkened her eyes. "See something that interests you?"

He shrugged. "Have you located Daddy Worthington or is he still living it up in the Caribbean on what's left of your inheritance?"

"Your rumors were right on target." She clasped her hands together and placed them gracefully on her lap. "He seems to have disappeared."

"Along with his nineteen-something plaything?"

Laurel frowned. "Why are you doing this? What did I do to deserve—"

"Why did it take you so long to tell me about the baby?"

She stared at him, her features composed. Ever the heiress. "My mother needed me. There were debts to settle, things to sell."

"I'd say notifying me about the baby was as important as any of those other things."

"Did you forget how to dial a phone? You knew I was pregnant. Why didn't *you* contact *me?*"

Brett didn't answer.

When he'd returned from Reno, he'd picked up the phone more times than he wanted to admit, but he couldn't bring himself to call her. She knew how to contact him if she wanted to. As the months slowly passed without a word, he'd realized the obvious. Laurel had thought she was too far above him to call. It hadn't been the first time it happened to him. But after he'd heard mutual "friends" joking and snickering about her finances and pregnancy, he'd hired a private investigator in Chicago.

Since then, he'd received daily reports on her activities. He had been about ready to step in, after learning her mother had lost the family estate, when he found out Laurel was heading via bus to Portland. To him. The P.I. had ridden with her the entire journey, just to ensure she arrived safely on his doorstep.

"I figured you'd contact me if you needed something."

"How diligent of you," she said.

"Seems we're both at fault." He rubbed his chin. "But your timing is interesting considering the article on me in this month's issue of *Forbes* and my book hitting the *New York Times* list."

"How dare you imply—"

He laughed at the indignant look on her face. "A Worthington to the end, aren't you? Even though the Worthington name is *worthless* thanks to your father and his reckless…style of living and loving."

"You make it sound so…sordid." She sighed. "Okay, it is sordid, but what's it to you?"

His gaze snapped to hers. "You're the mother of my child."

She stared down the length of her perfect nose. "Thank you for acknowledging the child as yours."

That "I'm-better-than-you" attitude made him want to toss her out of his office. But he couldn't. She was carrying his baby. He clenched his hand. "You were my wife."

"Our marriage was annulled, so we weren't really married."

He still found it hard to believe two total strangers could have ignited so much passion, so much longing, and parted company without so much as a business card exchanged. "How about my one-night bride?"

"How about we don't define it?"

"Fine."

Leaning her head back, she rubbed her neck. "Look, if I had anywhere else to turn…"

Here we go. What a pathetic joke. It was all he could do not to laugh.

Now she wanted him. Now that she didn't have two nickels to rub together, she would settle for someone like him. His jaw clamped.

Never had he imagined working so hard to build a successful life for himself, only to marry someone in a position far worse than he'd ever been in. He wasn't happy about what he needed to do, but it was too late for regrets.

Thanks to a roll of the dice, life as he knew it was over. But that wasn't an innocent baby's fault. Unless he took certain steps, the past was about to repeat itself. He wouldn't fail his child the way his own father had failed him. Brett had to do the right thing, the only thing.

He had to marry her.

His child needed a father; his child needed a family.

But before Brett offered marriage, he wanted *her* to say it. Ask for it. Beg for it. "Tell me what you want."

"I want...a job."

"Right. You traveled halfway across the country to ask me for a job."

"And to tell you about the baby." She bit her lip. "I didn't think it proper to tell you I was pregnant over the telephone."

She was worried about etiquette now? "What else?"

"Medical insurance to cover the pregnancy."

He'd fallen for her scam once before. Never again. He waited. She didn't say anything else. "That can't be it."

Her forehead wrinkled. "Why not? What more could I possibly need?"

His money. A band of gold on her finger. All of his money.

If only he could walk away...but he wasn't his father. Brett didn't have any other choice; he was in this for the long haul.

His gaze locked with hers. "That's really it?"

Laurel nodded.

If she wanted to play it this way, he was game. "Fine, I'll give you a job with a full benefits package. You'll supervise a small staff, organize and hostess events and perform philanthropic duties with various organizations throughout the city. You'll receive a top-notch health and dental plan. I'll toss in a clothing allowance and a car.''

''Sounds perfect.'' Her eyes sparkled. ''What's the position?''

''My wife.''

Chapter Two

Wife? He wanted to marry her? For real?

Her pulse picked up speed, and her dry throat got even drier. He couldn't be serious, but the intensity in Brett's eyes told Laurel he was.

She wet her lips, wondering what to say. Four months ago, she would have given anything to hear him propose marriage. Four months ago, she would have said yes without a second thought. Four months ago, she would have wanted him to bail her out of financial ruin.

But all that had changed. She had changed.

With a baby came responsibility—financial, moral, the works. She hadn't planned on having a child so soon or alone, but now that a baby was growing inside her, Laurel had to do right by her son or daughter. She wanted to be the kind of mother her child could look up to, respect. Not the kind of mother who needed handouts or a man to justify her existence.

Marriage wasn't the answer. Brett might be the father of her child, but she didn't need a white knight—make that a tarnished knight—to rescue her. She didn't need to be rescued by anyone except herself. She would make it on her own, prove to herself she wasn't like her mother.

"No," she answered.

His forehead wrinkled. "What did you say?"

"I said no," she repeated. "I don't want to marry you."

"You're saying no?" His eyes widened. "To me?"

"I don't see anyone else in the room." Laurel might not know much about Brett Matthews, but she knew she'd upset him. Okay, maybe not upset, but the way his dark brows furrowed told her that at the very least she frustrated him.

Good. He frustrated her, too.

She hated the way he studied her as if she were an annual report and he didn't know whether to buy or sell shares of stock. She hated him accusing her of getting pregnant on purpose. She hated having nowhere else to turn.

"Why?" he asked.

Where should she start? Laurel wasn't stupid. She knew the benefits of marrying a man like Brett. Financially she would be set, but Laurel had learned an important lesson from her parents: whoever controlled the purse strings controlled the relationship. It had even happened to her with her own father. She wasn't about to put herself in that position again. Especially with a man as wealthy as Brett Matthews.

Besides, *her* child didn't need wads of money, a trust fund or huge inheritance to be happy. Money was so transitory. Here today, gone tomorrow. Her child needed love and a positive role model for a parent. Those were the best things Laurel could give to her baby. "I don't want your money."

For the first time since she'd arrived, Brett laughed. "Do you expect me to believe you came all this way to get a job?"

"Yes, I do." Her calm voice hid the way she was seething inside. How could she have ever slept with him? He was the most aggravating, insufferable… She fought the urge to storm out of his office. Self-preservation kept her sitting with hands clasped on her lap. She really needed help getting a job. "If I wanted charity, I would have stayed in Chicago."

"I'm offering you marriage, not charity."

"Marriage for all the wrong reasons. I've already done that once. I won't do it again."

"I'm marrying you because the baby needs a father. That's reason enough."

"No, it's not." Sure she was pregnant with his baby, but Brett didn't even like her, let alone love her. Both her paternal grandmother and mother had married for money and position. Both had suffered when their roles as trophy wives came to an abrupt end. Laurel had already made the mistake of getting engaged to a man she didn't love. She wouldn't make an even bigger mistake and marry Brett. She wouldn't be like the other Worthington brides, who married for financial security and comfort. Baby or no baby. "No one *has* to get married these days."

His lips tightened. "People may think nothing about having a child out of wedlock these days, but that's not what I want for my baby. Marrying you is the honorable thing to do."

"Honor?" The word left a bitter taste in her mouth. Honor had died with her great-grandfather's generation.

"I know what you're doing, and I won't be an absentee dad. We have to get married. The baby needs a father."

"Says who?" She tilted her chin. "Lots of women raise children on their own. I can do it, too."

"You plan to raise the baby yourself?"

"Yes."

"What about a nanny? Someone to clean up all the messes and smells? Someone to take care of the baby while you're out, flitting about here and there?"

"My days of 'flitting about' are over." She touched her belly. "I love this baby more than anything. Dirty diapers, spit up and all."

A vein throbbed on his neck. "You could be the greatest mother ever, but a child still needs a father."

"Your point being?"

"Your baby *has* a father."

"Please. My baby has a sperm donor."

She met Brett's hard gaze with one she hoped equaled his. The line had been drawn.

"You're wrong, Laurel." He walked to his desk, sat and opened a drawer. Brett pulled out a pregnancy book. No biggie; she had a book of her own. Besides, it took more than reading to make a good parent. He removed two more. Next came three on child care. Brazelton, Leach, Eisenberg, Dodson, Gesell—the list of authors went on.

She shifted. "A bit premature, don't you think?"

"I believe in being prepared."

Okay, so he probably knew more about being pregnant than she did, but it wasn't that big a deal. He must be a man who had to know everything about every subject. But knowing wasn't doing. And none of that mattered right now. She was here for one reason and one reason only—to get a job. She couldn't let him make her forget that.

"See this?" He took out a file folder and waved it in the air. "Now that I know the truth, I'll have my attorneys finish preparing the necessary documents. Though they'll want a DNA test before making anything official.''

Papers? Lawyers? DNA?

Her heart fell to her feet and kept right on going. Forget about the job, even medical insurance. Brett had redrawn the line and hidden land mines in her path.

''You may be the one who's pregnant, but that baby is as much mine as it is yours. Don't ever forget that.''

Laurel couldn't lose control, not now. She wouldn't be able to afford to fight him if he wanted custody, but she'd sure as hell try. She hadn't been born on the Fourth of July for nothing. She would go out with a bang, fireworks and all. ''No test.''

''What?''

She was hungry and exhausted, and the initial adrenaline rush that had carried her to his office had vanished. With every ounce of strength she had, she stared him in the eyes. ''You either believe the baby is yours or you don't.'' Somehow she managed to keep her voice from shaking. ''If you want to sue for custody—''

''You think I would...''

She motioned to the file. ''Aren't those custody papers?''

He stared at her and frowned. ''It's my will.''

The air whooshed out of her lungs. ''I...''

''Is that really what you think of me?''

The hurt in his voice made her straighten in her chair. ''What am I supposed to think?''

''Anything but that. Our child needs a mother *and* a father.''

''This child will have both.'' She couldn't bring herself to say ''our'' child. Not yet, maybe not ever. ''We just won't live in the same house. At least I made the overture of relocating, which is more than I can say for 'Daddy.' ''

"I'm talking about a family, Laurel."

"A father doesn't make a family."

His nostrils flared. "I'll have to concede that point, but neither does a mother always."

Confused, she pushed her hair behind her ears. She hadn't come all the way to Portland to get a father for her baby and a husband for herself. Yes, she and Brett had shared a wonderful time in Reno. He'd been warm, gentle, caring, but they didn't love each other. She'd assumed he would help her find a job and make a clean start. She'd even thought he might be interested in the baby once he or she was born, but Laurel hadn't considered how large a role he wanted to play in *her* baby's life. That would make him a part of her life, too. Sharing a child, sharing memories, sharing a life...

"I have to go," she said, panicked.

"Where?"

"I...I need to get something to eat."

"I'll go with you."

"But—"

"Don't read anything into this. You need to eat, and I'm driving you. For the baby's sake."

For the baby's sake. Everything she had done so far had been for her baby, and nothing was working out. In fact, it was getting downright complicated. What was she going to do?

Brett was only trying to do the right thing. Why wasn't that good enough for Laurel? His family may not have crossed the Atlantic on the *Mayflower* or been listed on the pages of the social registry, but she was the desperate one, the one with no money, no home, no job. What would it take to convince her to marry him?

On the drive to the restaurant, the atmosphere in his car

was as chilly as a February morning, and the cold wasn't blasting from his air-conditioning. It didn't help matters that he recognized the scent of her perfume. A light floral fragrance he couldn't name, but the scent suited her perfectly and reminded him of how he'd watched her dress the morning after their so-called wedding night, how she'd dabbed the perfume behind her earlobes, on her wrists and in the hollow between her breasts.

He knew she'd thought he was asleep, and was trying to sneak out before he awakened. She hadn't known he'd been awake since dawn wondering what to do, what to say next. Laurel had taken care of that for him by leaving a note on the pillow next to him.

He'd read it so many times he had the damn thing memorized....

"Every little girl dreams of her wedding day, complete with her own Prince Charming. The wedding at the Love Dove chapel might not have met those expectations, but last night exceeded them. Thank you for making my dreams come true, even if it was for only one night. I wish I could stay longer, but family obligations require me to return to Chicago.
P.S. Thanks for the 'wedding' gift. I love the music box."

Sure she did. Brett knew better than to believe a word she said, either then or now. In Reno, he'd thought she would be the perfect wife. So much for perfection.

Yet he couldn't deny his attraction for her. An attraction that was growing by the minute. Hard as he found it to believe.

When they reached the restaurant parking lot, he helped her out of the car, and she stiffened at his touch. As he led her inside, his hand resting on the small of her back, she tensed. Enough was enough. This ice maiden routine had to stop.

But once they were seated and had ordered dinner, the tension between them didn't improve. The din of voices from the other diners' conversations and the sound of a piano from the lounge kept their lack of conversation from being overly awkward. A brush of her leg against his sent sparks flying for him, but she merely apologized, dismissing him without a thought, and took a sip of water.

Water wouldn't cut it for Brett. Three fingers of whiskey sounded about right. He wasn't much of a drinker, but Laurel could make a man do things he normally didn't do. He settled for beer, a local microbrew's award-winning summer ale, and tried to figure out his strategy.

He hadn't gotten this far by taking no for an answer.

Things weren't going as he expected—or rather, maybe they were. He'd deluded himself thinking Laurel could see beyond her upbringing and former station in life. Obviously, she couldn't.

He told himself he didn't care. This wasn't about her or him. The baby was the bottom line. His ego might be slightly bruised by her rejection of his offer of marriage, but he wasn't going to let that stop him.

She *had* to marry him.

His baby needed a family, and he would do whatever it took to make that happen. Even lower *his* standards to marry her.

"Now about us getting married," he said finally.

She massaged her temples. "Let's not repeat that mistake."

He flinched. "Mistake or not, I'm concerned how you intend to care for our baby."

"I already told you." She sighed. "Some women

choose to stay at home. Others choose to work. I'm going to work.''

''You're pregnant. You shouldn't be working.''

''Pregnancy is not an illness, though some nonintelligent people think it is. That's one reason I came to you.''

She really didn't have a clue. About life. About him.

''Don't roll your eyes at me, Brett Matthews.'' She pursed her lips. ''I didn't travel all this way on a whim. Do you think it was easy for me to leave my hometown for a city I've never been to? Do you think I wanted to spend three days on a bus?''

Everything she did surprised him. ''Why didn't you find a job in Chicago?''

She toyed with her napkin. ''I had a job, but it didn't work out.''

According to the P.I.'s report, she'd been fired from her job at an exclusive department store, but it hadn't said why.

''I looked for another job, but due to my father's stellar reputation always preceding me, I couldn't find anything that paid more than minimum wage. I thought you would be able to look past my current condition so I could start over and make a new life here in Portland.''

''You really want to work?''

''I really want to work.''

She sounded so serious. He found it hard to believe. The woman he'd been with in Reno had been a pampered heiress who didn't have a responsibility in the world. ''Do you have a degree?''

''A B.A. in art history.''

Not the most marketable degree to make a large amount of money unless she had artistic talent in the field of counterfeiting. ''Any special skills?''

''I'm a good shopper.''

"Your one skill is to spend money?"

"Don't frown, it's a skill and helped me get a job. I worked for two weeks as a personal shopper at a department store. I was good at it, too."

"What happened?"

"I got fired," she admitted. "It was a combination of things. Tiredness, tardiness, morning sickness. One day I didn't make it to the bathroom in time. Needless to say, in spite of receiving a brand-new pair of Pradas, my customer wasn't pleased. Neither were the higher ups at the store, and it was the last straw considering I was only a trainee, not a full employee."

"Have you worked any other jobs?" He'd bet before the stint at the store, she'd never had a job in her life. She probably lived off her daddy's credit cards. "After graduation, in college, high school?"

She stared at her glass of milk. "No, but I'm great at planning parties. I've also chaired several charity events."

No wonder she couldn't find a job in Chicago. Laurel Worthington had no marketable skills.

"There has to be a job for me somewhere."

How could he hire her for a real position? Yet he saw how determined she was to find a job. Something he'd never considered her wanting to do. "How much money do you have left?"

She hesitated. "Enough."

He doubted that. If she had enough, why had she pocketed two dinner rolls when she thought he wasn't looking? "Any assets?"

The edges of her mouth turned up slightly. "Do my suitcase and bag count?"

There. He saw it—a glimpse of the fun-loving socialite he'd wedded and bedded in Reno. "Are they filled with family heirlooms, jewels or works of art?"

"No, some clothes, a few things for the baby and a couple knickknacks." The momentary light dimmed from her eyes. "I liquidated everything to pay the creditors."

"Why didn't you file for bankruptcy? Your debts would have been forgiven. You might have been able to keep your condo and your car."

"I'm not my father." Her lower lip quivered and she took a deep breath. "I take responsibility for my problems, not catch the first plane to the Caribbean. I don't want my baby to grow up thinking Worthingtons run away when times get rough or take the easy way out. I have to do it right. My name is the one thing I can give to the baby."

The baby is a Matthews, too. But Brett realized it hadn't occurred to her yet. "What about your mother?"

"She's living off the generosity of friends in hopes of finding a husband who will support her and her spending habits."

"You could learn something from her."

"I have." She raised her determined gaze to his. "And I'm not about to forget it."

Maybe Laurel had learned more from her mother and grandmother than she wanted to admit. The strained civility with Brett was too reminiscent of the final days before her father took flight. Yet Laurel had said nothing. She'd controlled her temper and allowed Brett to take the lead when dinner arrived.

She knew the reason. It had been months since she'd eaten in a nice restaurant, and she'd been too hungry to let the tension bother her. But she had to admit it was strange and disconcerting.

The romantic setting—flickering candlelight, sweet-smelling fresh flowers, soft music—contradicted what was really happening between them. They weren't a couple on a date, but two strangers sharing a meal and polite conversation. Avoiding what needed to be said. Ignoring what they'd shared once. Pretending they hadn't created a baby together. Laurel was only too happy to pretend.

But now that her stomach was full and the plates cleared, it was time to get down to business.

"It's getting late." She leaned toward him. "Are you going to give me a job or not?"

"I'm sorry, but—"

"But what?"

"You don't understand. I can't just—"

"Hire me?" Not wanting to cause a scene, she lowered her voice. "It couldn't be that hard to do. You own your own company."

"I run a business, as you so aptly pointed out. There are lots of organizations who will help you."

Charity organizations, he meant. So that's how he saw it. How everyone she knew had seen it, too. It was so easy to write a check or attend a five-hundred-dollar benefit in support of a good cause, but when it came to helping someone you knew... "Obviously, I made a mistake coming to you, but I thank you for your time." Only the knowledge that everything she owned was locked in his car kept her from walking out on him. She clenched her hands. "If you'd drop me off at Henry's on your way home, I'd appreciate it."

"Henry's in France."

How could she have forgotten that? Laurel pasted on a smile. "That's right, I don't know what I was thinking."

At that moment, the waiter placed the check on the table. Thank goodness. She didn't want to hear Brett tell her memory loss was a common symptom of pregnancy. Right now she had other concerns—such as where would she sleep tonight, when did the next bus head north and how far could she get on what she had left?

Both she and Brett reached for the check at the same time. "I'm not letting you pay," he said.

He wouldn't release his hold on the leather folder, and Laurel gripped tighter. "That makes two of us." She wasn't about to let him ease a guilty conscience by paying for dinner. She didn't want to feel indebted to him in any way. "Why are you being so difficult?"

He raised an eyebrow. "I'm the one who's being difficult?"

If only she had seen what he was really like in Reno. "Let go, please."

"You let go."

"You and I aren't on a date. In fact, we've never had a date. Just a wedding, a reception and great sex. Now we're having a baby. A relationship for the new millennium. Funny, wouldn't you say?"

Great sex? Laurel tried not to grimace. Had she really admitted the sex was great?

His gaze met hers and softened. "It was great, wasn't it?"

Why had she said that? Now he was going to get an even bigger head. She shrugged and tried to pull the check folder toward her, but it wouldn't budge. Brett Matthews was the most annoying, arrogant, chauvinistic man she'd ever known. "We can't sit here all night."

"Then let me pay and we can get out of here."

"I'd rather spend the night—"

"With me? I knew you'd come around eventually."

His grin took her totally by surprise. It reminded Laurel of their wedding, when he'd smiled at her as she walked down the aisle. In that moment she'd almost believed the wedding was real, with love and a happy future in store for her. That the marriage vows she would exchange would have meaning, that her groom would love her every day of her life and stay by her side no matter what.

For richer, for poorer.

A comforting warmth had filled her. A warmth that had lasted through the reception and grown during the elevator ride to the honeymoon suite. But it hadn't been real. Not by a long shot. She must have been delusional. Too bad she couldn't chalk it up to drinking too much champagne.

He chuckled. "I'll pay for dinner and then you can agree to marry me."

That did it. Brett might be tall, dark, handsome and rich—the type of man you wouldn't want to bring home to meet Mother because she would force you to marry him on the spot, or marry him herself—but Laurel wasn't going to take this from him.

"We'll go dutch." She released the check and whipped out her wallet from her purse. Her gaze lingered over the shrinking amount of money—only a few bills remained. Mentally, she calculated what her soup and chicken Caesar salad cost and added on a twenty percent tip. She should let him pay, but pride wouldn't allow it. Earlier, she'd stuffed a couple of dinner rolls in her coat pockets to make up for what she might spend tonight. Thank goodness Oregon didn't charge sales tax.

He snatched up the bill and tossed a credit card inside the folder. "I'm not letting you pay."

She shoved a twenty inside. She would have rather paid the exact amount, but she didn't want Brett to know how much—rather how little—money she had left. They sat in silence as the waiter arrived and left with the check.

"What are you trying to prove?" he asked finally.

"I don't want your charity or your money. Only a job."

"So you've said. But wouldn't giving you a job be considered charity?"

"No, because I'd work hard and earn every dollar you paid me. I'd do whatever it took to succeed. A win-win situation for both of us. But hey, it's your loss. Once I get to Alaska—"

"Alaska?"

She nodded. "Did you think I'd come all this way without a backup plan?"

The waiter arrived with Brett's credit card slip. He signed it, removed the twenty and tucked both the cash and the Platinum card into his wallet. "Why Alaska?"

"I used to watch a TV show set there. It looked like an interesting place. And I heard they pay you just to live there."

"What do you plan to do in Alaska?"

"Fish. I thought I could work on one of those fishing boats. You can earn a lot of overtime." She scooted out of the booth, and in an instant Brett was at her side, putting out his hand to assist her. Fed up, she refused his help.

Why did he keep touching her? Little impersonal touches that sent her blood boiling. She didn't like it one bit. All in all, it was better she was leaving Portland, leaving Brett. She couldn't afford to fall for him. Especially when she didn't even like the person he'd turned out to be. It might be harder to find a job somewhere else, but she could do it. Laurel touched her belly. She had the best reason in the world to succeed. "If you'll drop me off at the bus station, I'll be on my way."

"Isn't it a little late—"

"Buses usually run all night." Hoping buses departed at all hours and one would be leaving for Alaska sometime soon, she walked toward the exit. Before she could open the door, she felt Brett's hand on her shoulder. Not again. "What?"

"Forget Alaska," he said. "If you want a real job, you've got one at MGI."

Chapter Three

Brett couldn't believe he'd actually said the words, but the thought of Laurel leaving Portland had spurred him into action. The impulsive offer went against everything he believed in, but it was the only way to keep her nearby. He couldn't allow her to take his child away.

Her eyes widened. "You're serious?"

"Yes." He paused, trying to figure out what she could possibly do without causing any trouble or getting in the way. "My assistant has been telling me she needs help."

Laurel's smile widened. "You won't be sorry."

Brett hoped not. He only wondered what Debbie would say once she found out she was getting her own assistant. Perhaps she would be so excited she wouldn't demand a logical explanation, but knowing Debbie... He'd better call her at home. "I'll call my assistant tonight so she can make arrangements for tomorrow."

"I'll work really hard. You'll see." Laurel squeezed his hand. "Thank you."

At her touch, a jolt of awareness shot through him. The

warmth of her skin against his brought back memories of their lovemaking. And the way her hand lingered in Brett's told him she might be remembering, too.

Ending the handshake was the smart thing to do, but when it came to Laurel Worthington, logic failed him yet again. Hiring her was a perfect example, one he would have to discuss with his attorneys. Despite the circumstances, he couldn't deny his physical attraction to her, and the last thing he wanted to do was set the company up for a sexual harassment suit. Brett drew his hand away. "I only offered you the job. You won't report directly to me, so it'll be up to you to keep it."

"I'll be MGI's model employee."

She'd be lucky if she made it through the probation period. At least he could keep an eye on her at the office. Make sure she and the baby were doing well.

"What's my salary?"

"You can discuss your salary with your new boss."

She bit her lip. "I don't want to put you on the spot, but will I be paid more than minimum wage?"

"Everyone at MGI earns more than minimum wage."

"Great, because I need to be able to afford rent."

He couldn't imagine her living on her own. Maybe he should reconsider what to pay her, then convince her working for peanuts didn't make sense and she would be better off marrying him. An idea popped into his head. "Do you have a place to stay tonight?"

"I need to find a hotel. Nothing fancy. A motel, maybe."

Nothing expensive was what she meant. He wondered how much cash she was carrying around in her bag. Not much, he guessed. "You can stay with me."

"I—I don't want to be in the way."

A little late for that. "My mother fixed up the guest room and she uses it when she's in town."

"I don't want to keep her—"

He could tell Laurel was only searching for a polite excuse because she didn't want to stay with him. At least she was consistent. "She got tired of the rain and moved to Florida for some sunshine. It's yours. For as long as you need it."

"You make it sound as if I'll be there forever."

That's the plan. He had to convince her to marry him. Having her stay with him was the first step. Keeping her close was the second.

"I want to rent an apartment."

"I know, but this will give you time to get to know Portland and find the perfect place."

"Portland's not that big." She furrowed her perfectly arched brows as if she didn't know whether to trust him or not.

Welcome to the club, Ms. Worthington.

"Do you live near your office?"

"It's a short drive."

"Well, I wanted to stay close to the office, since I don't have a car."

"We'll car pool."

"Together?"

"That's the way it usually works." Brett smiled at his stroke of brilliance. Building his own business from nothing had taught him what it took to succeed—hard work and patience. The more time he spent with Laurel, the more opportunity he'd have to show her the benefits of marrying him. At home, at work, in the car. It was as good as done. He just needed to figure out what to do next. "Ready to go home?"

* * *

Home. The word conjured up so many different images—both good and bad—in Laurel's mind. Only the belt strapped across her lap kept her from sitting on the edge of her seat as Brett drove them along Highway 43 to an area called Dunthorpe. One of the more exclusive areas in Portland, she surmised, eyeing the other large houses in the older, established neighborhood, especially Henry Davenport's estate, which Brett pointed out.

As he pulled into his driveway, Laurel's heart pounded in her throat. The English-style manor had aged well and radiated warmth and family. The house was picture perfect and belonged in a painting, with blooming flowers and towering trees in the yard and gaslights illuminating the interior.

"I'll get your bags," he said.

Laurel made her way along the stone path to the entryway. With each step, she found herself falling in love with Brett's delightful house. The grounds, especially the carefully tended gardens, reminded her of the yard where she'd played as a child. The bittersweet memory reminded her of happier times—of the secure childhood she'd known as a young girl, and even recent years as an adult. She hoped Brett's yard only knew those happy days. Most likely it would. The yard was perfect for a child…a child who would visit once every week and every other weekend. The thought saddened her, and she shook off the feeling.

She should be relieved she had a place to stay tonight. In fact, it might even be nice to be pampered by his house staff.

As Laurel stood on the porch and waited for Brett, a moth fluttered around the light. Was she getting too close to the flame herself? Working at Brett's company was one thing, but staying with him? And wanting to be pampered? Her days of being pampered were over.

She shouldn't be here. Not for even one night.

All she wanted was a job and a chance to make it on her own. Not a marriage proposal, not a place to stay, not a ride to work every day. And she definitely didn't want her insides turning to melted butter with a simple touch of his hand.

Yet that's exactly what was happening. Being around Brett short-circuited her mind, her nerve endings, her heart. It wasn't real; it couldn't be, just some leftover attraction from the time they'd shared in Reno. But that didn't explain her roller-coaster swings of emotion. She wanted to laugh; she wanted to cry. She wanted to slap him; and for some insane reason she wanted to kiss him, too. It didn't make sense.

Must be the hormones.

At least she hoped that was all.

She couldn't risk anything else. Laurel had made her choices in Reno. She'd wanted one last weekend, one last time to be—or rather pretend to be—an heiress, who could have whatever she wanted, whenever she wanted.

Meeting Brett had been a welcome surprise. She'd never experienced such intense feelings or longing as she had when he'd kissed her during the wedding ceremony. She'd felt as if she'd won the lottery and had acted as if there were no tomorrow because, in her mind, tomorrow was an unknown quantity. It had been worth it because of the baby growing inside her, but now she had to think not only of tomorrow, but every day after that. Not just for her own sake, but for the little one she would be bringing into the world.

Would the baby have her blue eyes or Brett's brown ones? Would it be a boy or a girl? Laurel only hoped whatever sex their baby turned out to be, the child got Brett's money sense and his smile. She might not be thrilled with his personality, but she liked Brett's smile. A lot.

He carried her suitcase from his car, unlocked the front door and opened it. A beep sounded. "That's the alarm system. I'll give you the security code."

"I won't be here that long," she said a little too quickly. "I want to look for an apartment tomorrow. After work, that is."

"You may want to wait until Saturday. Then we can make a day out of it."

"We?" He'd suggested helping her get to know Portland, but Laurel assumed he was only being polite.

"I'll show you around and we can look at apartments, but I'd suggest memorizing the code unless you plan on spending all your time with me."

Memorizing the code moved to the top of her list.

He stepped inside and turned on a light. Laurel followed. The hardwood floors in the foyer gleamed from the light of the chandelier above. A wide staircase with an elaborately carved balustrade led to the second floor. So lovely. The faint scent of lemon—wood polish, perhaps?—lingered in the air.

She glanced to her right. The large room was dark, but it, too, had hardwood floors and... Oh, no. She screamed, "Call 911."

Brett dropped her suitcase with a thud and was at her side in a second, his hand on her waist. "What? Are you in pain? Is it the baby?"

"No, you've been robbed. They took everything."

All she could see was a fireplace. They'd even taken the lights. Tears welled in her eyes. She remembered her own condominium and her mother's house. Watching item by item being sold to strangers, seeing piece after piece being removed until only empty rooms and bare walls remained.

"Oh, Brett." She leaned into him and placed her hand over his, trying to give him what small amount of comfort she could. "I'm so sorry."

He moved away. "Everything's still here."

"Everything…?" She thought someone had stolen all his furniture. "Your living room is empty."

Not one of his muscles tensed. He didn't even blink an eye. "I haven't been robbed. I don't have any furniture."

She stepped into the cavernous room. In addition to the fireplace, piles of books were stacked against the far wall. "You're kidding!"

Brett shrugged. "I haven't gotten around to decorating yet."

"I'm sorry, I thought…"

She stared at the empty room and suddenly knew exactly where the Christmas tree would go. She pictured the miniature blinking lights. Not all white ones, but different colors of bulbs. An angel gracing the treetop. Greenery, candles and bows covering the wood mantel, along with a couple of those lighted porcelain village pieces. Velvet stockings, with names embroidered on them, hanging down. The smells of cinnamon and vanilla filling the air. And a crackling fire for the finishing touch.

"I usually don't have guests."

And this was one guest who needed to get out of here. The image forming in her mind was much too appealing. Laurel returned to the foyer. "How long have you lived here?"

"A year next month."

To her left was an empty formal dining room. No table, no chairs, no sideboard, nothing except a beautiful chandelier and more stacks of books on the floor. She stared in disbelief.

Every detail on the exterior of the house had been cared for with such precision. No one seeing the outside would ever think there was nothing inside. How could Brett live like this? How could he call this barren structure home?

"I had the floors refinished and the walls painted before I moved in. I spoke with a couple of designers, but I haven't had time to meet with them. One of these days, I'll get to it."

The neglected interior not only contradicted the exterior, but also the lavish and thoughtful decor of his office. "What about the person who decorated MGI?"

"She's known for her commercial designs."

"So? Anything has to be better than this."

The bare, stark white walls didn't belong in a home. The house was a blank easel wanting for someone to brush the first stroke of color.

So many questions filled her mind. Where did he sit? Where did he eat? Was she going to be sleeping on the floor tonight? Brett Matthews was becoming more of a mystery to her.

"Not every room is empty." He led her toward the back of the house to a kitchen-family room area. The family room consisted of a large stone fireplace with built-in bookcases on either side.

"See—" he gestured to a large-screen television, a leather recliner and a matching couch "—furniture."

Bachelor furniture was what he meant.

Dull, all-too-male.

This place needed a female's touch. A potted ficus would fit perfectly in the corner, and the spot over the mantel needed a painting to make it the focal point of the room. A small table and lamp against the wall, framed photos and other accessories for the built-in cabinets, and a nice rug to tie it all together… "Looks comfortable."

"It is." He pointed to a small alcove situated between the kitchen and the family room. A breakfast nook with a maple table and four Windsor chairs was surrounded by windows. "There's even a table."

Yes, but what did he eat? The kitchen was state of the art and immaculate. Either Brett was a neat-freak or he never cooked. She had to wonder if the Sub-Zero refrigerator contained any food. She knew firsthand not even a house full of servants could keep something looking so spotless and shiny-new looking. He must keep his staff busy if he wanted them to maintain that standard. "Very…nice."

But very strange.

If she didn't know better, Laurel would think no one lived here at all. There were no piles of clutter. No pieces of memorabilia. No character. Oh, the house had plenty of architectural character—beams on the ceiling, moldings, wood windows and floors, leaded-glass fronted built-ins, but that wasn't enough for a beautiful old home like this.

The house was crying out for some tender loving care, yet Brett had turned a deaf ear. His neglect saddened and concerned her. Was he superficial—showy on the outside, but empty on the inside?

The interior of his house only reaffirmed what she knew in her heart to be true—he really didn't want a family. Someone who lived like this wasn't interested in having a home, let alone a wife or child. He was a workaholic who preferred office comfort to that of his own house.

"Would you like something to drink?"

"No, thanks, I'm tired." She was ready to call it a night

and have her bed turned down. "Is your staff still on duty?"

"I don't have a staff. My housekeeper comes once a week."

"I just assumed…"

"I'm sure you did." He studied her as if he could read her thoughts and her dreams. "I'll show you to your room."

"Thank you."

With his hand at the small of her back, he motioned her toward the foyer, where he picked up her suitcase. "You have a private bath. Everything should be there. My mother is thorough when it comes to stocking guest rooms."

As Laurel climbed the stairs, a wave of apprehension swept over her. Brett, no staff, this house…she'd never expected to be alone with him here. It was getting stranger by the minute, and Alaska was looking better and better.

Following him to the end of the hallway, she noticed the lack of artwork, of anything on the walls. Where were the family pictures? Paintings that touched your soul and told you that you were home? Even a print or two would do.

Once again she was struck by the difference of his office. Which was the real Brett? Surely not the one so completely at ease in an empty mansion.

"There's a nice view of the Willamette from your room."

"The what?"

"The river that runs through Portland."

"Oh." She entered the guest bedroom and felt as if she'd stepped into another world. Exquisitely designed and magazine layout perfect. The classic combination of deep magenta and mahogany decor suited the English architecture. Unlike the rest of his house. Pictures in gilt frames sat on the dresser. One of a young boy and a woman—Brett and his mother? Another of Brett in a cap and gown.

"Make yourself at home. The dresser drawers are empty." He opened one of the closet doors. "I'll get more hangers once you send for the rest of your things."

"This is all I have left." The words left a bitter taste in her mouth, like a fine wine that had turned to vinegar.

"When you said they were your only assets..."

"It's okay. Really." She glanced around the room, not wanting to explain further. A crystal bowl filled with sweet smelling potpourri sat on the nightstand. "Your mother did a lovely job decorating the room."

"I'll tell her you think so. She enjoyed doing it," he said. "I told her to do whatever she wanted and create a home away from home for herself."

"Maybe you could ask her to do the rest of the house."

The scrutiny of his gaze made Laurel self-conscious. Finally, he looked away. "If you need anything, I'm right next door. Good night."

"'Night."

As soon as he left the room and closed the door, Laurel plopped onto the bed, feeling exhausted, dirty, confused. She blinked away the tears stinging her eyes. She'd come too far to break down and cry.

She rubbed her belly, seeking the reassurance touching her baby usually provided. "Sleep well, my little one. I have a feeling this is only the beginning."

And it worried her.

Nothing was turning out like she expected.

Not even Brett.

Still, Laurel couldn't forget the gorgeous man she'd met and married in Reno, the one who'd given her the sweetest wedding gift—a music box with two doves on top.

Had that been an act? Had he been pretending, too?

So many questions, too few answers.

Laurel kicked off her shoes. She needed a shower to scrub away the grime and whatever else was clinging to her. She would get a good night's sleep and be ready come sunrise. She couldn't forget....

Tomorrow her slate was wiped clean. Tomorrow she started her new job. Tomorrow was the first day of the rest of her life.

Brett knocked lightly on Laurel's bedroom door. There was no answer. He didn't hear any movement inside. Either she was still sleeping or she was in the bathroom getting ready. He hoped she was asleep. Waking her up before even roosters blinked would be a perfect way to start her day. His, too.

A morning to remember. He smiled, imagining what her reaction would be. He would have to be careful not to look too happy, but it would be difficult.

Today was the start of his get Laurel to say "I do" campaign. He'd spent half the night planning his new strategy. She'd thrown him a curve by turning down his marriage offer, but if making a name for himself in the crazy world of financial investments had taught Brett anything, he knew how to trench and regroup.

He would show her that working wasn't the picnic she thought it would be. Early, very early mornings, ten-hour-plus days—it wouldn't take long for her to see marriage was a better option, the only option. He would do nothing to affect her health and the baby's, but she might find herself more tired than normal and wanting to sleep in, nap, go to bed early. Looking for an apartment would be too draining. Doing anything would be too taxing. And he would be right by her side. To feed her, to listen to her, to comfort her.

If he played his cards right, she'd be ready to quit by this time next week. Brett grinned.

He knocked louder. Still nothing. He turned the knob and opened the door. At least she hadn't felt the need to lock it. That had to be a good sign. Maybe she would say "yes" that much sooner. "Laurel?" he called softly.

The even rise and fall of her chest told him she was still asleep. He walked toward the bed. She had kicked off the sheet and cotton blanket and curled up on her left side. Good, that was the position the pregnancy books recommended. One of those body pillows he'd read about might make her more comfortable, too.

Her oversize pink nightshirt skimmed the bottom of her panties. He shouldn't be looking, but he couldn't help himself. The dirt from her bus journey was gone, leaving the beautiful woman who had haunted his dreams these past four months. This was the woman he would spend the rest of his life—or at least the next eighteen years—with, the mother of his child.

He ran his gaze from her shapely legs to her stomach. He saw the slight roundness. Not much of a difference from the flat tummy he'd run his hands down and trailed kisses along in Reno.

But there was a difference.

His baby was in there. He touched her belly.

Laurel blinked open her eyes. He jerked his hand away before she had the chance to focus.

She yawned. "Brett?"

"Good morning."

She bolted upright. "I know I set the alarm clock for six o'clock. I must have slept through it. I'm sorry."

"You didn't sleep through the alarm."

"Then why…" She glanced at the east-facing window. Only the beginnings of daylight crept around the edges of the curtains and blinds. "What time is it?"

"Four-thirty."

Her eyes widened. "In the afternoon?"

"Four-thirty in the morning."

Her disbelief and look of utter horror made him smile. Good. That was the reaction he'd wanted. She'd probably never been up this early before. "I like to be at the office before the market opens. Is that a problem?"

"I…no." She rubbed her eyes. "You're already dressed."

"You were tired last night so I wanted to let you sleep in."

"How thoughtful of you." She looked at the digital alarm clock sitting on the nightstand. Another minute flashed by. "What time do we need to leave?"

"Half an hour, forty-five minutes. We can pick up breakfast on the way." He waited for an outcry. He didn't get one. "If you need more time —"

"I'll be ready."

Such certainty. "I'll be in the family room."

"See you in a few minutes."

Yeah, right. More like sixty minutes. Women like Laurel always took at least an hour to primp and pamper themselves. Brett left her room and headed downstairs. At least he could make use of the waiting time. He grabbed the remote control, turned on CNBC and sat in his recliner. He picked up his laptop and logged on to MGI's server. Time to slog through his e-mail.

In what seemed like record time, Laurel appeared downstairs. "I'm ready," she said. "If you need more time…"

He'd only had time for a few e-mails. He checked his watch. No way she could have gotten ready in less than fifteen minutes. "I was just logging off."

Brett looked up and his breath caught in his throat. He couldn't speak, he couldn't think. He could only stare. She was…stunning. His pulse started climbing faster than an Internet stock's IPO.

She wore a black above-the-knee skirt and a short-sleeved black shirt that fell below her hips and covered her stomach. A scarf tied around her neck added a splash of bright color. She'd piled her hair on top of her head and clipped it somehow. No bad-hair days for Laurel Worthington.

"Something wrong?" Meeting his gaze, she smoothed her blouse and skirt. "My wardrobe is somewhat limited with my expanding waistline, and I never was one for suits—"

"You look fine. Good. Great."

"Thank you." She smiled. "So are you ready?"

More than ready, Brett realized with a start. Ready to forget today was a workday and he needed to go to the office. Ready to pull the clip out of her hair and watch the silky strands come tumbling down around his hands. Ready to carry her up the stairs and to his bed.

Forget about not liking her, not respecting her, not trusting her.

He wanted her, wanted her bad.

Brett snapped his laptop closed. What the hell had he gotten himself into?

Chapter Four

What was wrong with him? Laurel couldn't figure it out, but ever since leaving his house, the only time she'd heard Brett say more than one word was when he stopped at a café and ordered breakfast to go. She'd told him she would prefer to stop at a grocery store—it would be less expensive than a restaurant—but he mumbled that there wasn't time and paid for her breakfast as well as his before she could protest.

She didn't know Brett well enough to know if this was what he was like in the morning. In Reno, she'd wanted to return home as soon as possible. Her mother needed her. But Laurel had also been afraid that the magic she and Brett had shared during the night would disappear come morning. She wanted the memory untarnished, something to keep close to her heart in the days that would come. So she'd left before he'd woken.

After seeing how he acted today, she'd been right to leave as she had. Obviously, he wasn't a morning person.

But nothing, especially Brett's strange mood, was going to interfere with her first day at work.

As Laurel stepped from the elevator, she noticed the crowd at the receptionist's desk. Even at this early—okay, ungodly—hour MGI bustled with activity. Investors or employees? She couldn't imagine who all the people were, but before she could contemplate it further Brett led her past the desk and through the door leading to the private offices.

Inside was just as crowded. What a difference from yesterday afternoon. People running about. Computers waking from a night's sleep. Telephones coming to life. The atmosphere vibrated with a contagious energy. Laurel smiled. She could almost taste the money being made.

Here, she could have a career. Here, she could make a name for herself. Here, she could earn enough to provide for her baby.

Her excitement mounting, she followed Brett down the hall. No one seemed to notice her, and for that she was grateful. No more covert looks, snide comments, tactless jokes. For once, she was glad to be a nobody. A fresh start was hers to make.

"I'll turn you over to Debbie," Brett said without a glance Laurel's way. "I have a full schedule today, but if you need something, she'll know how to reach me."

"I'll be fine." And Laurel knew she would be. This was why she'd come to Portland. She couldn't wait to get started. She could do without the early hours, but she was a working girl now and a soon-to-be mommy. Sacrifices had to be made, and she'd do whatever it took.

Brett entered an alcove to the right of his office. "Debbie?"

His assistant popped her head up over the cubicle wall and frowned. Gone was the bubbly, blond high school cheerleader from yesterday. "Morning, boss," Debbie said, no smile in sight.

"Good morning to you." Brett grinned. "You remember Laurel."

Debbie nodded.

He glanced at Laurel, but his gaze seemed to look right past her, as if she were invisible. "I have work to do so I'll leave you in Debbie's capable hands."

"Okay." But Laurel felt anything but okay. Tension emanated from her new boss. "Have a nice day, Brett."

"You, too." With that he disappeared into his office and closed the door.

Laurel waited for Debbie to say something, anything, but her new boss did nothing but stare. Laurel adjusted her tunic. She didn't have a basketball belly yet, only a small paunch, and she hoped people would think she was chubby, not pregnant. She never thought she'd ever think that way, but she wanted to pick the time to make her pregnancy public knowledge. "It doesn't look as if it's going to rain today."

Debbie shrugged. Obviously, she was less than thrilled with her new assistant.

No problem.

Laurel could handle this. Henry Davenport had always said she could charm the pants off a... She'd certainly charmed the pants off Brett in Reno. Now she had to charm Debbie. Laurel would simply give her boss a reason to smile. Surely by the end of the day she could achieve the small feat of one smile. She straightened her shoulders. "I'm excited about the opportunity to work for you."

Debbie blew out a puff of air. Not the most auspicious beginning.... "I guess we'd better get started. Have a seat."

Laurel sat and clasped her hands. Smile, she told herself. Whatever you do, keep smiling.

Debbie handed her a stack of papers. "You need to fill out these forms, then read the pamphlets about employee benefits and rights. Let me know if you have any questions once you're done."

Laurel stared at the two-inch-thick stack of papers and pamphlets on her lap. "I do have a couple of questions now if that's okay."

"What?"

She ignored Debbie's curtness. Maybe she was having a bad morning—not enough sleep, a fight with her significant other, that time of the month…. "What will my job be?"

"You're my assistant. You'll help me with my daily responsibilities. Answer phones, file, data entry. When another employee is out of the office, you'll fill in for them."

Sounded good to Laurel, and not too difficult, either. She'd be getting useful office experience. "I was also wondering about my salary? Brett said you would be the one—"

"Two thousand."

Two thousand a week? That was a thousand more than Laurel expected. She knew MGI was doing well, but…she did a quick calculation. Wow. She would be making six figures nearly a year earlier than she'd expected. She would be able to afford a nice two-bedroom apartment or condo. Stylish maternity clothes. A car.

It was all Laurel could do not to reach across the desk and give her new boss a hug. She rubbed her tummy instead. Things were really going to work out the way she thought they would.

Debbie glanced at a piece of paper. "Two thousand a month plus benefits."

A month? Laurel's yearly salary would only be… Her jaw nearly dropped open. Forget the nice apartment. Forget everything. It was more than minimum wage, but…

"Is something wrong?"

"Everything's…fine." Laurel forced the words from her lump-filled throat. She would make it. Somehow she could find a way to survive. She hadn't come all this way to fail.

"You'll be on a thirty-day probation period. Brett expects hard work, but he's generous when it comes to raises. There are six-month reviews, with annual salary increases. Occasionally, we'll get merit bonuses for a job or project well done. For the past five years, we've received year-end bonuses averaging ten percent of our yearly salaries. But that isn't guaranteed since it's based on company profits." Debbie gave a half smile. "Any other questions?"

How will I pay rent? Buy food and diapers? Cover the expense of day care? Overwhelmed didn't begin to describe how Laurel felt. She swallowed hard. "Not right now."

"Then I'll show you to the employee lounge where you can go over the materials."

Mustering all her strength, Laurel stood tall. She wasn't about to be defeated without a fight. "Lead the way."

Out of sight, out of mind. Brett wished the old adage were true. Forget the amount of work he needed to do. He found it difficult to focus. His thoughts kept drifting to Laurel. He wanted to see how her day was going, see how she was feeling, see her. And that surprised him, because he'd never expected to be so attracted to her again.

His attraction made zero sense considering what she had and was currently putting him through, so he made a conscious effort not to check up on her, but it was still one of the hardest things he'd ever done.

Brett glanced at his watch. Almost four-thirty. He usually worked until six or so, but it wasn't only him working anymore. Time to call it quits. He headed for his assistant's cubicle.

Debbie sat at her desk and typed on her keyboard, oblivious to everything but the rapid movement of her fingers and the words appearing on her computer monitor. Laurel was nowhere in sight. The collar of Brett's shirt seemed to tighten by the second. "Where is she?"

Debbie stopped typing and glanced up. "In the lounge."

Of course, where else would she be? He leaned against the desk. "How did it go?"

Debbie stared at her screen. "Okay."

She wasn't meeting his eyes. Debbie was usually more direct. Not a good sign. "Care to elaborate?"

She shrugged.

"What happened?"

"It's been…terrible."

Terrible was good. "That's great."

"Maybe for you." His normally happy and carefree assistant frowned. "I don't care about the bonus you promised me last night. I can't do this."

"Do what?"

"Be the boss from hell."

"Why not?"

"Because I'm not used to being mean and bitchy and making people cry."

"Laurel cried?"

"Almost." Debbie's eyes glistened, and for a moment he thought *she* might cry. "When she learned how much she would be making... I didn't know what to say. It's obvious she doesn't need the money. She's wearing a Hermès scarf, for goodness sake, and everything about her screams money. What is she doing here? Slumming?"

Brett laughed.

"This isn't funny. She might be your ex-wife, but she isn't mine. The only thing she needs is a hug, not a job."

"Exactly." Brett grinned. "And it's your responsibility to make her see that. What did you have her do today?"

"Read the employee information and fill out forms. Sort and open the afternoon mail."

"Too easy."

"She doesn't have a clue how to do anything."

"You need to teach her," he said encouragingly. Brett needed Debbie's help to pull this off. "We don't want her to do anything too strenuous, but you need to assign her the messy, dirty jobs. You know, the ones everyone puts off doing."

"No."

"Yes. Have her clean the coffeepot, load and unload the dishwasher and clean the refrigerator in the lounge. Stuff like that."

Debbie grimaced. "I didn't know you had such a mean streak."

"I'm doing her a favor. Besides, a little work will do her good." He chuckled. "I give her a week. Two at tops before she quits."

Then she'll be begging me to marry her. No doubt about it.

"And if you're wrong?"

"When was the last time I was wrong?"

"When you said on-line trading would never appeal to the average investor."

"We all make a mistake now and then," Brett admitted. "But I'm not wrong about Laurel Worthington."

"I hope not."

"Trust me."

Debbie studied him. "You're enjoying this, aren't you?"

"Not yet, but soon." Brett's grin widened. His plan would not fail. "Very soon."

How could it get any worse? Laurel had thought she'd reached rock bottom when a drunk stumbled onto the bus during a stopover in Spokane, Washington, and decided to take the seat next to her. But even then she could turn away from the stench and close her eyes. She couldn't even grab a catnap here at MGI. Never had Laurel thought she would prefer a bus ride to work.

But thanks to the combination of her aching feet, her too-tight panty hose and a tiredness she couldn't shake, she wanted to go to sleep and not wake up for a month.

What she wouldn't give for maternity clothes and a pair of low-heeled Italian pumps. A shopping spree. A day at a spa complete with a facial, massage and haircut, too. But when one made only two thousand a month…

She had to admit, Brett's marriage offer was looking better and better. Maybe he was right. Maybe she wasn't cut out for working. Maybe she wasn't any different from her mother and grandmother—trophy wives extraordinaire.

But marrying him meant giving up control over her life to a man who didn't love her. It meant giving up her dream of making it on her own and being self-sufficient. Of being a better person than she'd been before. Was she willing to do that in exchange for the fancy-free life of pampering and shopping?

Tempting, yes. But not when she had a child to consider. Her priorities had shifted. She couldn't follow in her mother's footsteps. Laurel dug her toes into the carpet.

"How's it going?" Brett asked from behind her.

She blinked open her heavy eyelids and turned. "Great." She couldn't muster up the right amount of enthusiasm, but managed a smile. "Did you have a good day?"

"It was busy, but I'm ready to call it quits." He touched the back of her chair. "How about you?"

Quitting time at last. She wanted to shout for joy. Instead, she shrugged. "I can finish this up tomorrow."

"We can look at a few apartments, then go out to dinner—"

"It's been a long day." Laurel wanted only to find her bed and crawl under the covers. "Could we wait until tomorrow or Saturday?"

"Okay." Funny, but he almost sounded disappointed. "What do you want for dinner?"

"Taco salad."

"I know a Mexican restaurant. I can make reservations—"

"I'd rather have the homemade kind, if that's okay."

"Uh, sure." He furrowed his brow. "But could you explain the difference between a homemade taco salad and a restaurant one?"

"It's not really different." Just thinking about it made Laurel hungry. Maybe she wasn't that tired, after all. "Same tortilla chips, ground beef, cheese, lettuce and tomatoes. But the homemade kind tastes better. And you can smother it with Thousand Island dressing. Yummy."

"Salad dressing?"

"The low-fat kind, of course."

"Of course."

She noticed the strange expression on his face. "Is that a problem?"

"No," he said. "We can stop by a grocery store on the way home."

Laurel rose from the chair slowly. Every joint hurt. Every muscle ached. And she'd thought a desk job would be easy. She rubbed her lower back.

With an anxious gleam in his eyes, he picked up her purse. "Are you okay?"

So maybe she was tired. Nothing some sleep—about twelve hours worth—couldn't fix. "A little stiff. I must have sat too long."

"Don't forget your shoes."

She glanced down at her feet and wondered how she would ever be able to squeeze them back into her shoes. What had possessed her to buy pumps with high heels?

"First days are always the hardest." The tenderness in his voice surprised her. So did his smile. "Tomorrow will be better."

It couldn't be much worse. Laurel sighed. "I'm counting on it."

Later that evening, Brett closed the door to the dishwasher and stared at Laurel lying on the couch with her eyes closed. He couldn't tell whether she was asleep or not, but he was worried.

His plan seemed to be working already, but maybe he'd gone too far. He only wanted to show Laurel how hard working would be, not have her get so exhausted. During dinner he'd thought she was going to fall face forward into her plate.

To make matters worse, she'd barely touched her food. "Can I get you anything?"

"No, thanks." Her voice was so soft, too soft.

Brett was completely out of his element. He was used to handling hundreds of millions of dollars and overseeing his own company and employees, but dealing with a pregnant woman, the mother of his unborn child... He didn't know where to begin, but he felt responsible. Responsible for Laurel's condition, her tiredness, the baby. Overwhelming was the only way to describe it. "Do you want something else to eat?"

She blinked open her eyes. "Dinner was great."

The circles under them had darkened. Maybe he should just carry her upstairs to bed. "You didn't eat much."

"I ate plenty."

Brett wasn't so sure. He sat on the end of the couch. "Tired?"

Her nod was barely perceivable. "I feel like I'm back in the first trimester. I was so tired and sick then."

He placed her feet on his lap so he'd have more room. "Morning sickness?"

She nodded again. "I now know why there are only children."

"That bad?"

"Twenty-four hours a day, seven days a week."

Laurel wiggled her toes and he noticed she'd removed her panty hose sometime between his cooking dinner and their eating it. He took her wiggling as a sign to rub her feet. The last time he'd touched her, they had been lying in bed, her bare back against his chest. She'd shimmied her shoulders when she'd wanted a massage.

"I thought I was going to die. Taking care of a baby has to be easier. That must be the reason pregnancy lasts so long."

Brett had no idea what taking care of an infant entailed. The books he'd read made it sound somewhat challenging, but people did it every day. It couldn't be that difficult. He rubbed the top of her left foot.

"I hope you didn't mind cooking dinner tonight."

"I didn't."

"Good, because there's just something about home cooking, don't you agree?"

He always ate out or ordered food to go. It was easier, with the hours he worked. But as long as Laurel was around, he'd better get used to cooking. Or hire a personal chef. "I do."

"You seem to know your way around the kitchen. How did you learn to cook so well?"

"My mother." Laurel's compliment pleased him more than he wanted to admit. At least it wasn't his cooking that had kept her from eating. He massaged her toes. "She used to make me sit at the kitchen table so she could supervise my homework. I'd do just about anything to get out of it, so I'd help her separate egg whites or chop vegetables. Pretty soon she had me help her prepare meals. I…we enjoyed cooking together."

"Really? My parents never even asked about my homework and as far as cooking, we had a cook who wouldn't let me near the kitchen."

When Laurel said it like that, the privileged life sounded rather cold. But he remembered Henry Davenport's parents. They must have been the exact opposite of the Worthingtons.

"That's too bad." Brett wouldn't have given up those times cooking with his mom for anything, even though most of the meals they'd prepared were for the Davenports. "Do you cook at all?"

"I know enough to keep from starving, but I couldn't

cook at the beginning of my pregnancy." She grimaced. "The smells. They were overpowering. You should have seen my mother when she had to let her staff go. She knew how to make coffee but that was about it. I'd reached a point in the pregnancy where I only wanted to eat things made with ground beef. Taco salad. Spaghetti with meat sauce. I learned how to cook fast."

Brett moved to her other foot. He didn't understand the appeal of ground beef nor the cravings associated with pregnancy. Even after the books he'd read he still found pregnancy a big mystery. He didn't think he'd ever understand what Laurel was going through. "What was it like when you first found out you were pregnant?"

"Terrifying."

Brett respected her honest answer even though he knew she didn't always tell the truth.

"I was pregnant and all alone. After a couple of days, the shock wore off and the excitement set in. I was still a little scared, but happy. So very happy." Her tired eyes came alive and danced. "It's amazing to know you have a life growing inside you, a life you made.... It's quite a miracle."

The enthusiasm in her voice brought a smile to his face. "What did your parents say?"

"My father was already gone. And my mother—" Laurel exhaled sharply "—she told me having a baby so young would ruin my figure. As if that was my biggest concern. She...tried as best as she could to be supportive, but the last thing she ever wanted was to be a grandmother. Being a mother was hard enough for her."

Laurel. Alone in the world. Brett couldn't believe it, but he actually felt sorry for her.

For a moment, neither said a word. The silence should

have been uncomfortable and driven a wedge further between them. But it wasn't, and it didn't.

That surprised him.

And worried him, too.

He rubbed her ankles, and she released a sigh. "Feel good?"

"If I were a kitten, I'd be purring."

He rubbed her arches and moved up her leg. Her skin was so soft beneath his fingers. "Did you know if you massage a certain area of the foot, you can induce labor?"

"Was that in one of your books?"

"Yes, it said—"

"Please don't talk." She closed her eyes. "What you're doing feels wonderful."

He continued the massage. She was sprawled out, half-asleep. His hands glided over her silky smooth skin. Rubbing her tired feet. Working out the kinks in her slender calves. Rewarding her for a long day at the office.

Laurel smiled. "I forgot how good you were at this."

He couldn't answer. Not when he was remembering the way she had trailed whisper-light kisses from his forehead to his chin, down his chest and lower. Her hands had rubbed, explored, aroused.

Different time. Different situation. Yet...

He couldn't forget how wonderful *she'd* made him feel in Reno. How her innocence, her eagerness, her curiosity had turned him on. How sitting with her at this moment felt so...natural.

"I was wondering," she said slowly.

His pulse picked up speed. His physical reaction to her was insane considering the circumstances, but he couldn't help himself. His hands moved up her calf. "What were you wondering?"

Raising her head, she opened her eyes and her gaze met

his. "Is it true you need to pay the first and last month's rent when you lease an apartment?"

He removed his hands. "What?"

"I need to know how much money it'll cost to rent a place."

"It depends on the landlord." Brett felt as if a bucket of ice water had been dumped on him. No problem. Time enough for more once they were married. No way would he settle for one of those in-name-only marriages. Not with a woman like Laurel Worthington. "Some require a security deposit, too. What did you do in Chicago?"

"After I graduated from college, I picked the condo I wanted, and my father did the rest. From the time I was little, he told me I had better things to do than waste my time and pretty head worrying about money." She frowned. "He took care of everything—bills, you name it. He went so far as to pick out my future husband, and I dutifully did as I was told and became engaged to a man I didn't love. Thank goodness we broke up."

Henry Davenport had mentioned something about her engagement being called off before the April Fools' bash in Reno, but Brett hadn't wanted to know any details then. Now he did. Badly. Before he could ask any questions, she continued on. "Big mistake, I know. But I can't blame my father completely for what happened. I was stupid. I went along with everything."

She was taking so much of the blame. Too much, in Brett's opinion. "You were young. You didn't know better."

"Thanks, but I'm hardly a kid anymore. I should have known better. I should have been more involved. But I never gave a second thought to what he did. Every year, I simply went on my way. I never asked to see any statements, any receipts, anything. And to think I wasn't the only one.''

"Your mother?'' Brett asked.

Laurel nodded. "And several of my father's friends, too.''

"Why would they trust him with their money?''

"My father is quite the charmer. He dreams big and talks others into believing it, too. He got lucky a couple of times, but he didn't know when to stop. He didn't understand the definition of risk. I guess I didn't, either.''

Speaking of which, Brett had reviewed her paperwork that afternoon, and her ultraconservative asset allocation for her retirement plan had raised a red flag. "Is that why you selected bond funds for your 401k?''

She nodded. "They have the lowest risk factor besides money markets.''

"They also have a lower return.'' He shouldn't be having this conversation with her. In the long run, it would be meaningless, but he couldn't help himself. Investing was in his blood; it was his life. He couldn't let her waste one day of potential gain. "You're only twenty-two.''

"I turned twenty-three on July fouth.''

Unbelievable. He hadn't even known her birthday. Most likely, she didn't know his. And they were having a baby together. "Either way, you're young and investing for the long term. You can afford to ride out market swings.''

"I'm finished taking chances. I'm tired of uncertainties. I only want guarantees from now on.''

"If only life were that simple…''

He felt much older than the ten years that separated their ages. She was so young, so vulnerable. And he was no better than her father, Brett realized with a start. He was trying to show her she wasn't cut out for the working world so she would marry him. A lump of guilt lodged in his throat and he swallowed hard.

But what was he supposed to do? Marriage was the best solution for everyone involved. Nothing else made sense. Nothing else would give their child the family he or she deserved.

Laurel stared at the fireplace, her gaze not really focused on anything. "Sometimes I wish…"

Her wistful tone tugged at his heart. "What?"

"That I could do it all over again and change the past."

He'd been there himself. More times than he liked to remember. "We all do."

"Even you?"

"Yes." Brett couldn't understand why he was opening up to her. He never talked about himself, not even to Henry, his nemesis and oldest friend. Brett shouldn't be saying anything to Laurel. "But we can't change what's happened. "

"I know. The past is the past." She looked up at him as if reading his mind and patted her belly. "Besides, I can't forget what's most important now."

He stared at her, then lowered his gaze to her stomach. "Neither can I."

Chapter Five

Laurel should have stayed in bed that morning. If she had, she wouldn't be in this situation. She wouldn't be sitting across the desk from her glaring boss. She wouldn't be in so much trouble.

But Laurel had gotten up because no matter how tired she might have been, she didn't have a choice. She had to take care of herself, pave a road for her baby's future.

Too bad she was doing such a lousy job.

"What were you thinking?" Debbie demanded. "Couldn't you tell the difference between a color toner cartridge and a regular one?"

Only the desk in her boss's cubicle separated them, but Laurel felt as if the entire Pacific Ocean stood between them, and ships had yet to be invented. She started to tuck a strand of hair behind her ear, then remembered the dark toner covering her hands. But dirty hands were the least of her problems. "I was only trying to help."

"You can explain that to Brett when I tell him we need a new color copier." Debbie slammed her palms against the desk. "And I don't know what he's going to say when he finds out all of the graphics for the reports were ruined."

Laurel knew exactly what he would say. She would be fired. No question about that. Not that she deserved anything less. "I'm so sorry."

"Sorry doesn't cut it. Those reports are for extremely important clients. They are supposed to be in the mail today."

"I…" At her boss's icy gaze, Laurel averted her eyes and stared at the desk. In a corner, she saw a miniature slot machine. It was only a toy, but it reminded her of Reno. The oxygen-infused casino air smelling like cigarette smoke and spilled alcohol. The melancholy melody drifting in from the piano bar. The flashing lights and clinking of coins at the slot machines. Memories—happy, sad and those in between—rushed back. The images, the emotions threatened to overwhelm her.

A lump formed in her throat; tears stung her eyes.

Not now, please not now.

But it was too late.

Laurel tried to blink away the tears filling her eyes, but she couldn't. Tears streamed down her face as if a levee had given way during a torrential downpour. She rose. "Please excuse me."

She walked briskly to the bathroom and stood at a sink. After a minute, the door swished behind her. A tissue appeared over her shoulder.

"Laurel?" Debbie asked. "Are you okay?"

No, she wasn't okay. She would never be okay again. She was incompetent and now everyone would know it.

"Hey, no one's perfect. We all screw up now and then." Debbie plucked another tissue. "I'm sorry if I came down on you too hard."

"That's not why…" Laurel tasted the salt from her warm tears. Oh, why couldn't she stop crying? She'd vowed never to cry again. Then to cry at work—on her second day at work… Pathetic.

"What's wrong?" Debbie asked.

"It's…complicated."

The door to the rest room opened, and Laurel saw the reflection of two women walking in. She looked away, but not before one, a beautiful Asian woman with waist-length black hair, caught a glimpse of her. "Hey, why all the tears?"

"It's complicated, CeCe," Debbie said.

The other woman, a brunette, stepped forward and touched Laurel's shoulder. "I'm Sarah, and this is Celia."

Celia smiled. "Friends call me CeCe."

"Can we help?" Sarah asked.

"I—I—I don't know." Laurel hiccuped. "I'm usually not this…this emotional."

"We've all been there." CeCe grabbed the entire box of tissues off the counter. "Why don't you tell us what's happening?"

"That sounds like a good idea," Sarah said.

Debbie stared at Laurel. "It's up to you."

Laurel could see the concern in all the women's eyes, especially Debbie's, but they were strangers. Co-workers, yes, but still strangers. Laurel hadn't even told her closest friends what was going on. Not that any of those people had truly been her friends, as she'd learned the hard way.

Sarah took her hesitation as a yes, and Laurel found herself sitting in the lounge area of the ladies' room, where two love seats faced each other. "So what's going on?" Sarah asked.

"I'm not sure this is such a good idea," Laurel admitted. "Brett might not want me to—"

"We won't say a word," CeCe pledged. "Will we, ladies?"

The other two nodded their agreement.

It had been so long since Laurel had talked, really talked to anyone. Not even her mother could get beyond her own situation to listen to her daughter's problems. Laurel had no one to talk to except her baby. She was lonely. Scared, too. "I don't know where to start."

"How about what made you cry?" CeCe suggested.

"I made her cry," Debbie admitted.

"It wasn't you," Laurel said. "It was the slot machine on your desk."

Sarah drew her brows together. "Why?"

"It reminded me of Reno."

"Reno?" All three asked at the same time.

Laurel wiped her eyes. "That's where Brett and I met and got married. It's where we, I…got pregnant."

Their eyes widened and their jaws dropped. Laurel hadn't meant to shock them, but it felt so good to finally say the words out loud. "Maybe that's why I'm so emotional," she said. "The hormones on top of everything else."

"Everything else?" Debbie asked.

"I'm not only unmarried and pregnant, but broke, too." Oh, no. A tear slipped down her face. Then another and another. "Brett thinks I got pregnant on purpose and am only after his money. Okay, I can see why he might think that. After all, my father did lose my inheritance and skip the country with what little remained and take his nubile, nineteen-year-old lover with him. And my mother is in the south of France sponging off her wealthy friends and trying to find another rich husband. But that doesn't mean I'm a…gold digger."

"Are you after Brett's money?" Debbie asked.

A fair question. "No," Laurel answered. "I'm not looking for handouts. The only money I want is the money I earn myself. Brett doesn't understand what I've been through, and I can't tell him because he'll just chalk it up to me being a poor little princess."

The three women stared at Laurel, their full attention focused on her. CeCe pursed her lips. "Has it been that bad?"

"Yes." It was such a relief to say what had been bottled up for so long. This wasn't the time or place, but it was too late now. Might as well get it all off her chest while she had the chance. "I liquidated everything to avoid bankruptcy, but when people found out it…changed them. Do you know what it's like to have your credit card cut in half in front of your friends?"

CeCe nodded. "That happened to me. It was so embarrassing."

At least Laurel wasn't the only one. She took a small amount of comfort in that. "One by one my friends stopped returning my calls, inviting me over. And my fiancé dumped me."

"You were engaged?" Sarah asked.

Engaged didn't seem like the accurate term for what she and Charles had been. Thank goodness it ended before any vows had been spoken. "My ex-fiancé was more interested in my money and family name than me. As soon as he found out I was broke, he asked for his engagement ring back."

"That is so brutal," Debbie said. "He didn't deserve you."

The other women nodded.

"Thanks, but I'm sure if Charles could see me now he'd be more than relieved. Not that I care what he thinks.

The only thing I care about is the baby growing inside of me. That's the most important thing in my world.''

"I know how you feel." Sarah smiled. "I'm a single mom, too. I'll be honest, it doesn't get any easier, but it's worth every struggle when you hold your baby in your arms."

"I'm sure it is." Laurel sighed at the thought of cuddling her own little bundle of joy. "But to tell you the truth, I'm a little worried about how I'm going to provide for a child. I always assumed I'd get married and be a stay-at-home mom like my mother, so I never learned anything about handling money. I've never balanced a checkbook. Not that it matters, since I don't have a check ing account.''

"You need a checking account," CeCe said. "Where will you deposit your paycheck?"

Laurel raised her toner-dyed hands in the air. "Look at me, I don't think I'll be getting a paycheck once Brett finds out—''

"You'll find another job," Debbie said.

"Why do you need another job?" CeCe asked.

"Because I broke the color copier and ruined a bunch of graphics for some important reports," Laurel admitted.

"You won't be fired for that." CeCe glanced at Debbie, who hung her head with an I-don't-know-what-he-might-do look.

Sarah patted Laurel's arm. "If that happens, we'll help you find a new job."

"I appreciate the offer, but I'm not sure how many people besides Brett would be willing to hire an unskilled worker who'll need maternity leave at the end of the year."

"It's against the law to discriminate against pregnancy, but your résumé could use some...developing. Still, everyone deserves a chance...." Debbie smiled one of her thousand watt grins. "Between the four of us, we'll figure something out. But first we need to get the toner off your hands."

Where could Laurel be? Dinner with co-workers had sounded innocent enough, especially when Brett learned Debbie would be going, too. A little outside-the-company-walls maneuvering by his faithful assistant, and Laurel would be more than willing to quit. But it was almost nine o'clock, and she still wasn't home.

Not only was Brett worried, he felt disappointed. He'd purchased several baby name books for Laurel. He hoped his small gesture would be the beginning of a bridge between them to show her they could be more than two strangers who had conceived a child, that they could be partners in this thing called parenthood.

If she would only come home...

Being alone in this big, empty house didn't seem as appealing as it had on Wednesday night, the night before Laurel arrived. Not even the pizza he'd had delivered or watching *Sportscenter* on ESPN made a difference.

What was wrong with him?

He had the perfect life. More money than he could ever spend, a house in one of the most desirable areas of Portland, a thriving company. But sitting on the couch last night, rubbing Laurel's feet and talking about her pregnancy had felt so...good. Better than it should, considering he and Laurel shared nothing except the bond of their baby. But they could have more. If only she would give him the chance to show her they could be a family...

The doorbell rang.

She's home.

Brett took his time reaching the foyer and pulled open

the door. Laurel stood in the entry, and relief washed over him.

"Hi." She sounded more chipper than he'd expected, considering the hour.

"Hi, yourself."

As she stepped inside, a horn honked. Laurel waved at the idling car. "Alex drove me home."

"Alex Niles?"

She removed her purse from her shoulder. "Yes, he seems to be quite the ladies' man."

One of MGI's rising stars, Alex Niles was a young hotshot, "handsome as sin," according to Debbie, and the last person Brett wanted Laurel spending time with. "I thought you were having dinner with Debbie and CeCe."

"And Sarah," Laurel said. "Alex helped us...pick a restaurant. He was working late so we invited him to join us. He offered to drive me home."

Of course he did, Brett thought, wondering how, without attracting too much attention, to tell the boy wonder to keep his hands off Laurel.

Brett noticed she didn't look as tired as last night. He wasn't sure whether that was a good or a bad thing. "Today must have gone better than yesterday."

She shrugged. "You could say that."

"Did something happen?"

"Why do you ask?"

"No reason." Something didn't feel...right. But he couldn't trust his instincts where Laurel was concerned. "Did you have a nice dinner?"

"Oh, yes." Laurel lay her purse on the kitchen counter then headed to the sofa. "I think I may have made some new friends today, too."

"Good." But it was far from good. Brett's concern level started to rise. He wanted Laurel to think of MGI

as a place to be avoided, not a place to meet friends and
have fun. "You just don't want to overdo it."

"I won't."

But staying out tonight had been a necessity for Laurel.
Thanks to Debbie, CeCe, Sarah and Alex, Brett would
never know about the broken color copier; he would never
know about the two hundred and fifty reports that had
been redone. Her new co-workers and friends had sworn
their secrecy, bought her pizza and saved her job.

Laurel plopped on the couch and kicked off her shoes.
"How was your evening?"

"Uneventful." He handed her a stack of gift-wrapped
presents. "I picked some things up for you."

"For me?" Surprised and touched, she stared at the
packages. "I…"

"Open them."

It had been so long since she'd opened anything new.
Her wedding night, when she'd received the music box
from Brett, to be exact. She unwrapped the first gift.
"Baby Names for the Millennium."

"I thought you might want to start thinking about
names."

"I love it. Thank you." Smiling, she opened the next.
A second name book. It felt like Christmas. She unwrapped the third and the fourth. More baby name books.
"Oh, Brett. This was so sweet of you. You don't know
how much it means to me, but one would have been
enough."

"One book is never enough."

She laughed. "Words to remember."

"Words to live by."

Laurel found it hard to speak and clutched one of the
books against her chest. "I've been going through this
pregnancy alone. No one cares…."

"I care." Brett's compassion shone in his eyes, and a warm glow flowed through her. "I'm not looking to be a figurehead, Laurel. I want to be a real father. Not only when the baby's born, but now. Like you said, there's a life growing inside you, and I helped make it, too."

For the first time in a long while, she didn't feel so alone. Tears pooled in her eyes, and she smiled. "I see that." And she did. He truly cared, and for that she was grateful. She relished the thought of having someone to share the wonders of her pregnancy with. "There's, uh, something I wanted to ask you. I...it's time for my monthly OB visit. I made an appointment today with a doctor Sarah recommended, and I was wondering if you wanted to..." Feeling oddly nervous, she stared at the floor. "Never mind, you're probably busy on Monday and—"

"You'd let me go?"

She looked up. "If you wanted...."

"I do," he said. "What time on Monday?"

"Two o'clock, but if that isn't okay with you—"

"I'll rearrange my schedule."

"Really?"

Brett nodded.

"Great." And it was. It was also a good start to seeing how they would handle being parents together. She handed him one of the name books and grinned. "Start reading, Daddy."

His eyes widened. "Daddy?"

She nodded. "Like you said, it's your baby, too."

He grinned. "Yes, it is."

As she started skimming through her book, he opened another and read. Several minutes later, she felt his gaze upon her.

"What do you think of Emma?" Brett asked.

"It's pretty." Laurel flipped to the popularity chart at the back of her book. There it was. "But it's popular, especially among yuppies."

"Forget that one. Maybe we should start a list."

Was he going to be picky about names? She smiled at the thought. "Okay, but we still have a long way to go."

"What about Amelia?"

"That's a nice name."

"I think so, too." He returned to his book.

Seeing him concentrate so hard as he read through the pages of baby names made Laurel feel all warm and fuzzy inside. They might not be able to make a close, loving, traditional family, but the baby would have close, loving parents. It was more than she'd had. Laurel wondered about Brett. "Were your parents close?"

He glanced up from his book. "Why do you ask?"

"We know so little about each other. I'd like to know more about you and your family."

"My mom's the greatest. She can do anything she sets her mind to. She taught me to throw a curveball and kick a field goal. She's also an ace at geometry. She worked really hard when I was growing up, but she was always there when I needed her."

Laurel could tell how much Brett's mother meant to him from the way his voice and eyes softened as he spoke about her. She imagined he'd be the same with the baby. "And your father?"

"Never knew him. Never knew his name, what he did, what he looked like, where he was from." Brett shrugged, but from the way his mouth tightened and his eyes narrowed, Laurel could tell he was far from indifferent. "He ran out on my mother when she was pregnant with me. She never mentioned him. It was just me and my mom."

"I'm sorry, Brett. I had no idea." No wonder being a

good father was so important to him. Laurel touched his shoulder. "I'm really glad you told me."

"There's something else you don't know." Brett looked away. "My mother was the Davenports' house-keeper. We lived in an apartment above their garage until I graduated from college."

Laurel stared at him, seeing him for the first time. "So when Henry said the two of you grew up together, he really meant it?"

"I've known Henry since I was born. But I was never part of his 'gang.' Just the housekeeper's bastard son."

"You're so much more than that." Laurel smiled. "You're an incredible man, Brett Matthews. You should be proud of yourself." She was.

He slanted her a glance. "Why would you say that?"

"Look at how far you've come," she said. "You weren't handed a trust fund and set loose in the world. You made something of yourself. All on your own. That counts for a lot in my book."

"But not enough for you to marry me."

"Is that why you thought I said no?"

"Old money and new money don't mix."

"In case you forgot, I have no money." She grinned. "And I don't care about your past."

His lips tightened. "Would you say that if you hadn't lost all your money?"

"I can't answer that." Though she wished with every fiber of her being that she could. "I do know I'm not the same person I used to be. Even after everything I've been through, I think it's a good thing. No, I know it's a very good thing."

His surprised gaze met hers. "Then why did you turn me down?"

She hesitated. "Because I want to be like you."

"Like me?"

The puzzled look in his eyes was cute. He didn't get it, but Laurel realized that was okay. She smiled, happy to share a sliver of her dream with him after he'd shared a bit of his past. "You went against the odds and made it on your own. You showed the world that nothing was beyond your reach. I want to do that, too."

"You can do that and still be married."

"I can't," she said. "Not after what happened with my parents. I want—need—to be a person my child can be proud of, look up to. The way you look up to your mother. I need to provide for the baby myself and make it on my own. Do you understand?"

"I think so, but do you understand how badly I want our child to have a family?"

"I do," she admitted. "But there are no guarantees that a family will be together forever. Just look at me and my parents."

"But the alternative... I know how difficult it is to grow up without a father. My mom did the best she could, but it wasn't easy for her to be a working, single parent."

"Times have changed."

"Not that much," he said. "Talk to Sarah if you really want to know what it's like to be a single parent today."

Laurel knew the reality. She wasn't living in a dreamworld. "Sarah told me there were some hard times."

"That's putting it mildly." His eyes filled with worry. "It's not something I want for my child. Or for you."

"I appreciate the concern, but I can do it."

"I don't want you to have to 'do it.' I don't want the baby to go through what I went through."

The pain in his voice pierced her heart. She couldn't imagine what he'd been through. "Was it that bad?"

He nodded. "Do you know what it's like to grow up

envying your closest friend? Henry Davenport had the greatest dad in the entire world. I would sit and watch them. They were always doing something together—golfing, reading, playing. I was so jealous. I thought if only my father had stuck around, I could have all that Henry did.''

Everything was becoming so much clearer to her. Too bad Brett couldn't see what she already did—that he would be the kind of father he wished he'd had whether she married him or not. She wanted to touch his face, soften the hard set of his jaw. But she couldn't. They didn't have that kind of relationship. Not yet. Most likely never. ''Oh, Brett.''

''I don't want my child to feel the way I... It's important for me to give my baby the most and the best I can.''

''That's wonderful as long as you remember what's most important.''

''And that would be?''

She pointed to her heart. ''Love.''

''Love doesn't put food on the table or a roof over your head.''

''True, but children don't think about those things. At least I never did,'' she said. ''Even though you didn't have everything Henry had, did you ever question your mother's love?''

''Not once,'' he said without the slightest hesitation.

''Then you were rich in the truest sense of the word.''

Laurel shifted on the couch, and her book tumbled from her lap. She reached for it at the same time as Brett. Their hands touched. Their faces were mere inches apart. Brett glanced up and some of his hair brushed her cheek. ''You really believe that, don't you?''

''I really do.'' Her words sounded a little hoarse.

Forget about whatever they didn't agree upon. He

smelled so good. A mix of soap and something she couldn't define as anything other than male. The scent of him made her want to take a deep breath and never exhale.

She finally convinced her brain to move her hand away from his. He picked up the book and gave it to her. He didn't say anything, but the warmth of his breath caressed her neck. She could barely think, let alone speak.

She expected him to back away, to retreat to his corner of the couch, to do anything but stay where he was. But he stayed as if spellbound. Not that she was doing any better herself.

She wet her lips and parted them. Brett took it as an invitation and lowered his mouth to hers. When their lips met, an electric shock jolted her.

Jackpot.

Seven-seven-seven.

Bells whistled, lights flashed, the slot machine bucket filled with silver dollars.

She opened her mouth further, wanting to soak up the taste that was purely his. The texture, the heat...

His tongue explored, ravished, tortured. It was pure heaven, it was pure hell.

His hands splayed across her back, pulling her toward him, and she was helpless. She wanted to be closer, much closer and inched toward him until she was practically on his lap. He felt so good, so warm, so strong.

His arms offered the sense of security she hadn't felt since their night in Reno. The security she wanted to pretend she didn't need. And she didn't want to stop.

She wanted one last taste, one last feel of him. Kissing Brett made her forget everything, made her feel so carefree. A way Laurel hadn't felt in months.

She wanted him.

She wanted the magic they'd shared in Reno.

She wanted it to be real.

But as the last piece of reality started to abandon her, he pulled away.

"I'm sorry," he said, his breathing ragged, his eyes stormy. "I don't want you to think I'm putting the moves on you, but there's still some sort of...chemistry between us."

Understatement of the year. Not trusting her voice, she nodded, trying to catch her own breath.

"If you and I...we... If we were married—"

"But we're not, and we never will be." Laurel said the words, but they didn't come out as forcefully as she might have hoped.

He said nothing, but a vein pulsed in his neck.

She was confused, confused over what she felt for him. Brett made her feel sexy, alive, but also safe. Was that her attraction to him? Surely it wasn't anything real. It couldn't be. He didn't love her. And she didn't love him.

Brett picked up the books from the floor and set them in a stack on the table. They must have fallen during the kiss. She hadn't noticed. Truth be told, she wouldn't have noticed if the walls collapsed. Dangerous, Brett was too dangerous. Too attractive. She had to keep her distance. "We shouldn't do this again."

"All right." He drew his lips into a thin line. "We'll just go to bed."

Bed? With her? Surely she misunderstood, but her pulse rate accelerated, her body betraying her mind. "Excuse me?"

"You had a long day and need to sleep."

What she needed was a cold shower, not sleep.

"Don't forget, tomorrow we start looking at apartments."

Laurel only hoped she found one. The sooner she got away from Brett Matthews, the better.

On Sunday, Brett sat in the breakfast nook with Laurel, who poured over the classified ads. A day and a half of driving around Portland and looking at apartments had more than discouraged her. It was exactly what he'd hoped for; he'd wanted to show Laurel that life with him was the best choice.

So why did he feel like such a creep? Like he was trading on insider information?

"I can't believe those are the only apartments I can afford. A dingy studio with a fire-hazard kitchenette in an awful area. And I used to think staying in a four star hotel was roughing it."

That about summed up what he'd shown her. He'd skipped the better parts of town she could afford. It was for *her* own good. "Rent is expensive."

She frowned. "There has to be something…a way to make this work. Other people do it. I just don't understand how. What am I not getting?"

He told himself to play it cool. He was about to close his position, lock in his profit. And yet… "If you make a budget and save your money, you'll be able to afford more."

The words were out of his mouth before he could stop them. Never mind the conflict of interest. Or that he wasn't furthering his own cause.

She gave a dejected laugh. "I don't know how to do anything with money except spend it. I wouldn't be able to make a budget let alone stick to one."

"It's not that difficult."

What the hell was he doing?

She looked up at him. "You know all about this stuff, don't you?"

Uh-oh. He saw a glimmer of hope in her eyes. "Well, I..."

"Oh, Brett, I don't think I could stand it if I lost everything I had again or had to live in one of those smelly apartments we saw." She put her right palm over her heart. "I need to learn how to deal with my finances. Would you help me set up a budget and teach me how to manage my money—what little I have, that is—so I could save enough to afford a decent apartment?"

Good going, Matthews. The idea's to get her to stay, not help her leave, in case you'd forgotten.

"Please?" Her eyes held such hope and promise.

And what if he turned her down? She'd have nowhere to go. He realized in that moment he didn't want Laurel to bend to his will because she had no other choice. He didn't want her to settle for him out of sheer desperation. He wanted her to choose him, of her own free will, because he was her best choice. And the only way she could make any choice was from a position of strength. He had to help her get there.

Teach her to manage her money, show her she could succeed at whatever she set her mind to. The only question was how?

And then it hit him. His house.

He could have Laurel turn his house into a home. A home she would want to live in some day.

"I have an idea." Brett hoped he wasn't making the biggest mistake of his life. "What if I helped you with your budget and you helped me decorate my house?"

"You mean a trade?"

"Exactly. Modern day bartering."

"Well, I did decorate my father's pied-à-terre." Her

eyes visibly brightened. "It came out quite nice if I say so myself." She stared at Brett. "You'd really trade with me?"

"I've got something you want, and you…" She had a lot he wanted. More than a lot. "You could stay here—"

"I could pay rent."

"Actually, since you'd be taking on a bigger task than me, I'd give you room and board to make it a fair exchange. That way you can save money for an apartment, and I get a house where I can invite people over. We both win."

"And you only want me to decorate the house. Nothing more."

He heard a twinge of wariness in her voice. "We won't be playing house, if that's what you mean."

"I just want to be clear. No love or marriage or anything like that."

"None whatsoever." Once she reached her goal, he would reach his. "An even trade. What do you say?"

Chapter Six

Laurel stood in her room and stared at her suitcase. She'd been putting off unpacking all afternoon, but it was time to face facts. She was going to be living with Brett. Not forever, but for some time.

This wasn't a setback, she told herself, but a stepping stone for her and the baby's future. Yes, she still had a ways to go, but she was going to make it on her own. She could do it.

And she would.

Opening her bag, she stared at the jumble of contents. She removed a tissue-covered frame and unwrapped a photo of her family—her mother, her father and herself. Laurel had been ten at the time, the apple of her parents' eyes. They'd been so happy at the time of this portrait. How could life have gone so wrong? How could her father have walked out on them? Broken their hearts? Left them to clean up his mess?

She already knew Brett would be a better father than hers had ever been. Brett truly cared and wanted only the best for the baby. He wouldn't taint his child with his misguided beliefs the way her own father had.

Laurel removed a picture of her and her mother. *Worthington women always survive.* Her paternal grandmother had told Laurel that on her sixteenth birthday. Laurel hoped Grandmama was right. Not only for her own sake, but her mother's, too.

Next she pulled out the music box—her wedding present from Brett—and turned the knob. The wedding march played. The two doves on top spun as their nest turned.

This simple gift reminded her of the most magical night of her life. She still found it hard to believe he'd given the music box to her. She'd seen it in the lobby of the wedding chapel. Somehow Brett must have seen her admiring it, because the music box was waiting for her when they arrived at their honeymoon suite.

Laurel opened the top. Inside the royal-blue folds of satin lay the tacky boulder of a ring from the Reno wedding ceremony. It was cheap and cheesy—a bad imitation of the real thing, like their one-night marriage. Yet Laurel couldn't bring herself to get rid of it. The wedding ring was also a reminder of her few stolen hours with Brett. The night might have been pure fantasy, but it was her fantasy. One she never wanted to forget.

Staring at her still-full suitcase, Laurel closed the music box. Time to get busy. She wanted to get started on Brett's house. Not only for his sake, but the baby's, too. Her little one would be spending lots of time here.

Laurel touched her belly. "You'll love your daddy's house once I get done with it. I promise you, Junior, it'll be the perfect home for you and him."

She hung up what was left of her designer wardrobe. The rest had gone to high-end consignment stores in Chicago to finance her trip west. Anything loose-fitting she'd kept in hopes of wearing during the pregnancy, but even those clothes were getting tight.

A knock sounded on the door. "Laurel?" Brett asked.

"Just a minute." She slid the music box under a pillow, uncertain if she wanted him to know how much his present had come to mean to her over the past months. "Come in."

"I wanted to check on you." He opened the door and entered the room. "You were so quiet."

"I'm fine." Deep in her heart, she knew she would be, too. She motioned to the empty suitcase on the bed. "I've been unpacking."

"That's great." His dazzling smile took her breath away, but as quickly as the smile appeared, it disappeared. A good thing, she realized once she had a moment to think about it. His eyes darkened. "It must be hard living out of a suitcase."

She nodded, even though she knew there were worse things than that, especially when it came to having a place to live. She would never again take having a roof over her head for granted. "But I don't have to live that way any longer. Speaking of how we live, I thought we could start discussing your preferences for the house. Colors, types of furniture. Things like that."

"Do what you want."

She planted her hands on her hips and glared at him. "You agreed to help, or have you already forgotten?"

He sighed. "I thought you weren't paying attention."

"I always pay attention."

"I'll have to remember that." Mischief gleamed in his eyes. "And I'll have to watch what I say."

"You do that."

"Well, if you're going to force me to participate, I know which room I want to start with."

Laurel smiled. "Now that's the spirit."

He led her into another bedroom across the hall. It wasn't as large as hers, but had its own bath, too. "What do you think?"

Hardwood floors, high ceilings. Very nice, but no one would ever see this room. "It's lovely, but why do you want to start here?"

"It's going to be the nursery."

The nursery. She curved her arms around her belly, closed her eyes and visualized the finished room. A rug on the hardwood floor, a rocking chair near a bookcase, a changing table and crib, a bunch of stuffed animals and toys. She opened her eyes. "It's perfect, Brett, absolutely perfect."

"I was hoping you'd think so." He smiled. "My bedroom's across the hall. I want to get a baby monitor and install a video camera monitoring system so I can see the baby when I'm downstairs."

Her baby would have a really good, caring father. A bit overprotective, perhaps, but Laurel took comfort in the thought. Time to get her act together herself. She needed to start reading more, learning what mothers everywhere knew. "You've thought of everything."

"Not everything, but—" he moved to one wall "—the crib could go here so we could peek in without the baby seeing us. And the changing table could go right next to the bathroom...."

She bit back a laugh. "You have lots of ideas for someone not interested in decorating."

Brett shrugged. "This is different."

"Yes, it is." Excitement shone in his eyes and the smile plastered on his face kept getting bigger and bigger. Happiness and joy bubbled up inside of her. "Thanks."

"For what?"

"For caring. For taking the time to think about what would be good for the baby and…" She hesitated. Suddenly, she felt so different. All tingly inside. A little tongue-tied. "It means a lot to me…and Junior here."

"Junior?"

She hadn't meant to call the baby that in front of Brett. Her cheeks warmed and she looked out one of the wide windows to the yard below. "Sometimes I, um, talk to the baby. I call it different names, since I don't know if it's a boy or a girl. It's probably silly, but talking to the baby makes it seem more real. It's too soon to feel the baby move, and I've only heard the baby's heartbeat once."

Brett moved toward her. "What did it sound like?"

"Whoosh-whoosh-whoosh." The memory brought a smile to her face. "It was really fast, but…"

"What?"

"Since the morning sickness got better, I don't always feel pregnant and it…worries me. I mean, my stomach's getting bigger and I know there's a baby growing inside, but I don't always feel like there is." Sharing her fears felt almost as intimate as the kiss they'd shared on Thursday. "Silly."

"Not silly at all." He extended his arm toward her belly. "Is it okay if I…?"

Nodding, she held her breath.

He touched her stomach with his fingertips. Gently, with reverence. After a moment, he rested his entire palm on her belly. "Listen to Daddy, Junior. I know you're moving around in there, but could you make it a little more obvious so your mommy won't worry so much?"

Laurel smiled. "That's so sweet."

But there was nothing sweet about his hand on her body. Heat radiated from his touch through the fabric of her blouse. She wondered if his handprint would be seared on her skin. Not that she cared, but she should. Laurel shouldn't want him to keep touching her like this, but she did.

His gaze met hers, and her heart seemed to stop beating.

For a moment, she could almost believe they were a couple, a family. Better watch it, Laurel cautioned herself. Brett made it easy for her to forget nothing romantic would ever develop between them. But a little more of this and Junior would be the least of her worries.

Monday afternoon, Brett unlocked and opened the car door for Laurel in the parking lot of the medical office building. They'd finished the appointment with Dr. Miles, and Brett was completely in awe. He still couldn't believe what he'd just heard. Or that Laurel had shared this with him, no one else. He felt so close to her at this moment.

"One hundred and fifty beats per minutes." Hearing his baby's heartbeat made everything seem more real. The baby wasn't just something to talk about, it was alive. Someone was really in there, a little person. "Can you believe how fast Junior's heart was beating?"

"Pretty amazing." She smiled and got into the car.

"I'll say." It was the most wonderful sound he'd ever heard in his life. He walked around the car, slid into his seat and closed the door. "What did you think of Dr. Miles?"

"He's everything Sarah said he would be. I think he'll be good." Laurel fastened her seat belt. "What about you?"

"He seems thorough," Brett admitted.

"I didn't realize they would take blood again. They did during my first appointment in Chicago. Routine tests, this time."

The alpha-fetoprotein test, or AFP. He'd read about it in one of his pregnancy books. During the visit, Brett had felt as if he should be taking notes. He wanted to know everything that was going on so he could be ready for anything that might happen during the pregnancy. But he'd felt honored to be included at the appointment and didn't want to be in the way, so had kept his mouth closed. At the next one in four weeks, he'd be better prepared. Though he wished it were sooner. Laurel would be having an ultrasound then. Brett sighed. He couldn't wait. Four more weeks until they got to see the baby. A real image of Junior. A picture for his desk.

After buckling in, Brett glanced at his watch. Two-thirty. Plenty of time to return to the office and put in a few more hours, but the last thing he wanted to do was work. The market had already closed. His staff could handle after-hour trading and put out any fires if they erupted this afternoon.

He turned the ignition on the car and the engine roared to life. "Want to get some ice cream?"

Laurel did a double take. "What did you say?"

"I asked if you wanted to get ice cream."

"Don't we need to get back to work?"

"No, we don't." He smiled. "I'm the boss, remember."

"I can't believe you want to play hooky." She eyed him cautiously. "And you want me to, too. What kind of example—"

"No one will know."

"I'll know."

Brett gripped the leather covered steering wheel. "I just heard Junior's heartbeat for the first time. Don't you think that deserves a celebration?"

"When you put it that way…" A thoughtful smile appeared on her lips. "I do love ice cream."

"Mint chocolate chip."

Her eyes widened. "You remembered."

"I remember everything, Laurel."

She blushed. "Everything?"

Brett nodded. He shouldn't be bringing this up, but he couldn't help himself. "Did you think I could forget?"

"I…" She wet her lips. "I hoped you wouldn't."

"I haven't." His gaze captured hers, and the memories rushed back. At three in the morning, she'd wanted a bowl of mint chocolate chip ice cream. Thanks to a hundred dollar tip, a bellhop delivered Laurel's favorite ice cream along with chocolate sauce, whipped cream and cherries. The ice cream had melted before they'd gotten the chance to eat it, but the condiments had been put to good use. Brett had never looked at an ice cream sundae the same since.

"Let's celebrate." Her eyes twinkled. "I want at least two cherries. And nuts. Lots of nuts."

He smiled, happy she was getting into celebration mode, too. "After the ice cream, we can stop at a couple of baby stores and see if we can get ideas for the nursery."

The appreciative look in Laurel's eyes made him feel warm inside. *Watch out,* a voice cautioned him. That was the last thing she should be able to do, but he ignored the warning. She flashed him a dazzling smile, and he wanted to shout, "Victory!"

"You sure know the way to a girl's heart," she said.

Brett's grin widened. This was only the beginning.

Sitting in his office a few days later, Brett scanned the last of his e-mail for the afternoon and closed his laptop.

Time to call it a day.

He and Laurel were settling into a comfortable routine. And Brett enjoyed it. Enjoyed going home at a reasonable hour. Enjoyed her companionship and conversation. They'd prepare dinner, eat and chat about their day, the house, managing money and whatever other topic happened to come up.

The daily routine and endless amount of time spent together made it seem as if they were already married. At least that's what he assumed married life would be like. Of course, marriage implied a physical relationship, which was something definitely lacking between them. He hadn't tried to kiss her again, but it wasn't easy. A little physical contact would be nice. Maybe once he felt the baby move, he could use that as an excuse to get closer to her, to touch her. He was willing to try anything, which was part of his growing problem.

He was in over his head, and there wasn't a damn thing he could do about it. He wanted to show her how much they could have together, how much he could give Junior. But it was too soon. Talk about frustrating.

As he taught Laurel how to manage not only her own money, but the decorating account he'd set up, he saw how much she needed to learn. He blamed her ignorance about the value of a dollar on her parents, who had sheltered and insulated Laurel from the realities of day-to-day living and finances.

And that made it harder for Brett. Damn hard, to be honest.

She was so young, so naive when it came to everyday life. The last thing he wanted was to help her succeed in becoming self-sufficient. He wanted to keep her safe from a world that would gobble her up and spit her right back out. But he couldn't. He had to help her succeed, teach her to stand on her own two feet. That was the only way he could get what he wanted.

"Are you busy?" Laurel asked from the doorway of his office.

"No." He closed his briefcase. "I was about to come find you. I'm ready to leave." As she stepped inside, he noticed her lower lip tremble. "What's wrong?"

She said nothing, but curved her arms around her belly. "Th-the baby."

The baby? He rose from his desk and moved toward her. It was all he could do not to demand she tell him what was wrong.

Her eyes glistened with tears. She blinked. Once. Twice. The room was so quiet Brett thought he heard the fluttering of her eyelashes. "Take your time."

"I just got a phone call from Dr. Miles," she said finally.

"And?" The word came out too fast, too harsh. Brett wanted to smack himself. *Remain calm, Matthews. In control.* "What did the good doctor say?"

She bit her lip.

The fear of something being wrong with Junior, with Laurel, tore his insides apart. He couldn't imagine what it could be, but he was scared. More so than he'd ever been in his life. This wasn't about some stranger, this was about his child. Every passing nanosecond felt like a year and made his gut ache. He'd never experienced anything like it, and never wanted to again.

"The test results came back…" Her shaky voice faded and she took a deep breath. "He wants me to see a geneticist."

Brett tried to comprehend what she was saying.

"I'm at risk for Down's syndrome."

Down's syndrome and Junior… No amount of money could heal a genetic problem. He'd never felt so helpless. But this shouldn't be an issue at her age, the rational side of his brain told him, and logic set in. Numbers he could deal with. Emotion, forget it. "The risk can't be that high at your age?"

"One in 109."

"That's less than one percent."

"It's still considered high." She blinked again. "Dr. Miles recommended I have an amniocentesis." A single tear fell from her eye. "Oh, Brett, I'm so scared. If something's wrong with the baby…"

He wrapped his arms around her. He'd forgotten how soft and warm she was, how perfect she felt against him. How holding her felt so right. A way he'd never thought it would feel again.

When she hugged him back… He drew comfort and strength from her touch, and he wanted to stay like this forever.

No matter what. They were in this together. "The baby will be fine."

"What if it's not?" Her voice cracked. "What if—"

"We don't know enough to think like that." He said the words for both their benefits. Yes, he was worried about the baby, but he had a bigger concern. Laurel. Frightened and upset, she needed him to be strong. She might want to be independent and self-reliant, but right now she needed him as much as he needed her.

Together they would face what needed to be faced. Together they would get through this. Together…

Tears streamed down Laurel's face. Seeing her cry tore his heart in two. He struggled to think of something, of anything to say to make her feel better, but he couldn't. That made him feel worse.

She wiped her eyes. "What am *I* going to do?"

"You're not in this alone." Brett, Laurel and Junior. They were a family. He took a step back, raised her chin with his fingertip and gazed into her eyes. "Don't forget, you have the baby—" he kissed the top of her forehead "—and you have me."

At twelve-thirty in the morning, Laurel headed downstairs. She'd gone to bed at eight, but all she did was toss and turn and cry into her pillow so Brett wouldn't hear her sobs.

She'd even pulled out her music box. Hearing the wedding march play, watching the doves spin and thinking about her baby had been her salvation during the dark days in Chicago and had kept her going...all the way to Portland, Oregon. All the way to Brett. And tonight it had kept her from falling apart completely.

Still she couldn't turn off the emotions surging through her—the desolation.

Although Brett was being as supportive as possible, she still felt isolated. Alone. Yes, this affected him, too, but the baby was growing inside of *her*. Whatever might be wrong was wrong inside of *her*. No matter how hard Brett tried, no matter what he said, he couldn't change that.

Her stomach grumbled. Food should be the last of her concerns at a moment like this, but she couldn't forget she was eating for two.

Laurel rubbed her tummy. "Mommy should have eaten more tonight like your daddy said." She sniffled. "Are you as hungry as I am, little one?"

She thought of the tiny baby in her belly. Once again, tears threatened to fall. She rubbed her eyes. Junior had changed her life, changed her—made her grow up and accept responsibility. It was time to be strong for both her and the baby's sake.

No more falling apart.

Whether or not something was wrong with the baby didn't change the facts. She was going to be having this child. Come what may. There wasn't any other choice for her. She wondered about Brett and what he might be thinking. It would be so much easier if he loved her and she loved him. But that wasn't the case....

As she entered the kitchen, she heard a clicking sound. Sitting in his recliner, Brett worked on his laptop. He glanced up. "Hungry?"

She nodded. "And thirsty."

He set his laptop on the floor and walked to the kitchen. "I'll warm up a plate of leftovers for you."

"I can do it."

"I will." He opened the refrigerator, pulled out a plate covered with plastic wrap and placed it in the microwave. "I knew you'd want something to eat eventually, so it's ready to go."

She sat at the table. It felt strange to go through the motions as if they were a pair of robots. "Thanks."

"Did you sleep?"

"A little."

He raised an eyebrow.

No matter how much she might want to hide the turmoil inside her, it was futile to try with Brett. Though they hadn't known each other long, he still seemed to know her well. "Not much."

"I couldn't sleep, either."

"I can't stop thinking about Junior."

"Me, neither." He poured a glass of milk and handed it to her. "I'm also worried about you."

"I'm...fine." She said the words, then realized how

unreasonable they sounded given the circumstances. No doubt her eyes were red and swollen from her crying. "I'll be fine once we know...I mean..."

"I know what you mean."

She took a long hard look at him and noticed the mixture of weariness, worry and fear in his eyes. He was suffering as much as she was, and her heart cried out to him.

"I've been doing some research on the Internet," he admitted. "The AFP is only a screening test to tell you the percentage of risk. You should see all the posts on false positive tests. If you want me to show you what I found..."

"Thanks, but—"

The timer dinged. Brett removed the plate. "What?"

She took a sip of milk and set her glass on the table. It was time for complete honesty. "I've been doing a lot of thinking."

He placed a fork, napkin and the plate on the table. "Sounds serious."

It was. When she first arrived in Portland, she'd said he was nothing more than a sperm donor. Then she came to think of him as the baby's father. What was he now? Would he really stick by her and Junior through thick and thin?

"It doesn't matter what the test results or the geneticist say, I'm having this baby." As she patted her belly, her love for the baby coursed through her. "I love Junior. He or she is the only family I have left, and the number of chromosomes won't change the way I feel. I...I thought you should know."

He exhaled deeply. "I wasn't sure what you were going to say, but I realized whatever you decided, I would stand by your decision."

Even though his support made her happy, Laurel's muscles tensed. Did he really want the baby if it was less than perfect? Afraid to ask, afraid to discover the truth, she took a bite of spaghetti.

Brett sat at the table. "But I'm so relieved."

She held her fork in midair. "Relieved."

He nodded. The tightness around his mouth eased. "Forget about what the tests say, I want this baby so much it hurts."

His sincerity brought tears to her eyes. A welcome peace settled in her heart. "This is one thing I'm happy we agree upon."

"Me, too." One side of his mouth curved up and he leaned back in his chair. "Since the test results won't change what we do, we can skip the amniocentesis. Did you know that?"

"Yes, but…" Laurel moved food around on her plate. She shouldn't feel so uncertain about how he would react, not after what they'd already shared. She looked up at him. "I still want to have it. I know there could be…complications, but after everything that's happened these past months, I need to know. Knowing won't make a difference, and I'll love this baby no matter what, but I don't think I could relax during the rest of the pregnancy with that uncertainty hanging over me." She sighed. "I'm not making any sense, am I?"

"You're making perfect sense to me."

"And you're being very nice." And supportive and understanding and caring and… She needed Brett right now. More than she'd ever needed anyone or anything in her life. "Do you mind if I go ahead with the amnio?"

"Not at all. I think you should." His reassuring tone made her feel so much better. "Who knows what my father passed on to me?"

"That never entered my mind, Brett."

"But it entered mine." With a faraway look in his eyes, he rubbed the stubble on his chin. "I'll fly your mother in from France. I can book a seat on the Concorde—"

"No," Laurel said a little too quickly. "Thanks, but I'd rather you didn't."

He said nothing, but questions lingered in his eyes. It would be easier for her to change the subject. She couldn't. She didn't want him to surprise her and fly her mother out anyway. Laurel had to tell him the truth. For both their sakes. "There's something I haven't told you about my mother."

"You don't have—"

"Yes, I do." Laurel wet her lips. "When my mother found out I was pregnant, she told me to…get rid of the baby. If she thought for a minute the baby wasn't one hundred percent healthy… In any case, I don't want her here, and I don't want her to know the test results."

Reaching across the table, Brett held Laurel's hand and stroked her thumb with his own. His warmth seeped into her, filling up all the places that needed to be filled. "I'm sorry." His voice was so tender, practically a caress.

"Thanks." She stared at her fingers engulfed in his. His hand was so much larger, stronger, yet his gentle touch offered comfort, provided a safe haven.

Right now being part of a family sounded better than all the independence in the world. She wished he could see how much they could have together if they loved one another. Too bad she couldn't pretend the security she felt with Brett was more, that it was real and they could all be a family.

"Is there anyone else you want to go with you to the amnio?" His gaze met hers, and for a moment she felt a flash of the magic they'd shared in Reno. If only they could hold on to that...forever. "Tell me who, and I'll—"

"The only person I want with me—" she squeezed his hand "—is you."

Chapter Seven

The waiting room at the prenatal diagnostic center was empty except for them. Shifting in his chair, Brett wondered if Laurel was as nervous as he was. He felt as if he were a tennis racket strung too tightly and could only imagine how she felt. He didn't want to ask, because they seemed to have reached an unspoken agreement over the past few days—no talking about the upcoming appointment.

All their spare time had been filled with decorating the house: looking at furniture, samples of fabrics, paint chips. They'd even hired an interior designer, Renée Bernard, who promised to limit her creative input unless asked. Renée would help Laurel order furniture and coordinate painters, craftsmen and deliveries.

Brett wasn't sure if not speaking about the test was working, but they were making great strides in ordering items for the house, and Laurel seemed to be managing the decorating budget without any major problems. At least one thing was going better than he expected.

"Can I get you anything?" What he really wanted to do was hold her, cradle her in his arms and comfort her. But something held him back.

Laurel handed him her empty water bottle. "A bucket."

"You just drank the water." One look at her unsmiling face told him she wasn't kidding. "Don't tell me you have to go already?"

"You try drinking thirty-two ounces of water and see if you don't have to go." She crossed her legs. "I don't know how I'm going to last until the ultrasound."

"You can do it." The meeting with the geneticist would take about an hour, then the ultrasound would be followed by the amniocentesis. "If you want, I'll drink the same amount of water and suffer with you."

For the first time all morning, she smiled, a real smile that reached all the way to her eyes. "That goes above and beyond the call of fatherhood, but thanks. I appreciate the thought."

Brett wanted to snap a picture of her at that moment and save it for the wait after the test. But he knew he'd have to rely on his memory. Something that was easy to do when it came to Laurel. "If you change your mind..."

"Don't worry, I won't." She fidgeted in her chair. "Let's hope they aren't running late."

Within a few minutes, the geneticist, who introduced herself as Kathryn Lake, called them. As they followed her to an office, Laurel slipped her hand in Brett's. He was so surprised he almost stopped walking. But he continued forward, both relieved and grateful for the contact. It was the first time in days she had touched him, and it felt so good, almost too good the way her hand fit so perfectly in his.

Inside the office, Kathryn handed them each a business

card. She looked much too young, with her flowing red hair and clunky heeled shoes, to have all those initials behind her name. But as she explained how the AFP screening test worked and what would be done today, Brett realized Kathryn knew her stuff. He only wished she would get on with it. No doubt Laurel was uncomfortable, and he couldn't wait until all this was over and they could go home. He'd arranged for both of them to take the afternoon off, with strict orders to his staff not to phone or page him unless the market crashed.

"I reviewed the questionnaire you filled out and didn't see anything out of the ordinary, but it's routine to take a family history." As Kathryn asked Laurel about her family history she drew it on a piece of graph paper. One shape, a circle, for Laurel, then above that two more representing her parents. "This is you, Brett." Kathryn added a triangle next to Laurel's circle. "How is your health?"

"Excellent."

"What about your mother?"

"She's never sick."

"Excellent health, then." Kathryn drew another shape to the right and above his. "And your father?"

Brett hesitated. He should have asked his mother. He should have... A wave of insecurity washed over him. He was no longer a successful financial advisor, but a scared little boy trying to take on all the bigger kids who were calling him names, making fun of him and his mom.

One glance at Laurel, and Brett regained control. Her respect and unwavering support gave him strength to ignore all the bad memories churning in his brain and simply tell the truth. "I don't know anything about my father."

Kathryn didn't question him or look at him funny or

say a word. She merely jotted a note next to a shape and continued on. "Any brothers or sisters?"

"No, but I don't know about any half siblings."

"That's fine," Kathryn said. "Any cousins, aunts or uncles who may have had any birth defects."

"Not that I know of."

"Okay." Kathryn showed them the graph she'd compiled and explained how she looked for possible inherited disorders. Once finished she led them into the ultrasound room and introduced them to the technician, Rex, a tall man with a short ponytail.

The room was dark except for a light mounted underneath a cabinet and the glowing buttons on the high tech machine and the monitors. The only noise was an electrical hum. Laurel situated herself on the table, pulled up her shirt and tucked the waistband of her leggings under her belly. It was the first time Brett had seen her stomach. Even though she was lying down, he noticed a difference. He recognized the smooth skin and cute belly button, but her tummy was no longer flat. He knew she was pregnant, but seeing it with his own eyes—it was all he could do not to reach out and touch....

Rex squirted clear jelly onto Laurel's stomach. He pushed a couple of buttons and the monitor to the left of her came to life. Using a wand, he touched her belly. An image appeared on the screen.

The baby.

Their baby.

Brett could hardly breathe. He made out the head. Junior's head. *His* baby's head. His knees went weak and he grabbed on to the table for support.

"This is the skull," Rex said. "No water on the brain, hydrocephalus. That's good." He pointed to thick lines on the monitor. "See the ventricles?"

Brett glanced at Laurel, who stared wide-eyed at the monitor. "I can't believe that's our baby." Her voice was full of awe. "Do you see Junior, Brett?"

"I do." He grinned, happy to be sharing this moment with her. Forget what could be wrong. Junior was right there on the screen, heart beating and moving. That's all that mattered. "It's incredible."

More amazing than when the DOW first broke 10,000. More amazing than hearing Junior's heartbeat. Brett couldn't imagine what actually holding the baby would feel like, but he couldn't wait to find out.

"There's the spine and you can see the vertebrae." Rex pushed more buttons. "Are you uncomfortable, Laurel?"

She looked at Rex. "I'm...okay."

"Well, I'm not, and I'm just looking at how full your bladder is." He used a towel to wipe the gel off her belly and handed her a paper cup. "I want you to fill this up two times, then come back."

"Only twice?" Her voice rose an octave, and she looked horrified at the thought. "You're kidding, right?"

"No," Rex said. "And you don't need to bring the cup back."

"Don't worry, I won't." Laurel left the room.

Brett continued to stare at the image on the screen. Hearing the heartbeat had been incredible, but this...he wanted to sit and let it all soak in. Seeing the baby made impending fatherhood seem that much closer. Doubts assailed him. Suddenly all the books he had read, and was reading, didn't seem enough. How would he know what to do? What to say?

"Is this your first child?" Rex asked Brett.

"Yes." Together he and Laurel had created this life. Now they had to create a family. Surely she would realize how important it was for them to marry.

"It's an exciting time. Even if you decide to have another child, there's nothing like seeing the ultrasound for the first time."

Another child? Both he and Laurel were only children. He didn't want that for Junior. Brett wondered what Laurel would think when she found out he wanted more than one. He'd better wait until the ring was on her finger and Junior in her arms before he broached that topic. "Do you have kids?"

"Two. A boy and a girl." Rex pointed to a picture on the wall. "That's them."

"Cute kids."

He nodded. "There's nothing like being a parent. No one can tell you what it's like. You have to experience it to believe it."

Brett couldn't wait. Couldn't wait until Junior was born. Couldn't wait to experience all the "firsts." First bath, first step, first word, first birthday, first bruise...

His stomach knotted. How had his mother ever done it on her own? And how could his father have walked away without a second thought? Having a child was overwhelming. The responsibility, the time commitment, the worry. But the rewards...and the love...

Brett glanced back at the image frozen on the monitor and was overcome by an onslaught of emotion. *You'll never be uncertain of my love for you, Junior. Never.*

As Rex continued the ultrasound, he rattled off technical terms about high resolution Doppler something or other, but Laurel wasn't interested in the medical terminology. She was interested only in the image on the monitor.

Seeing her baby floating inside her, the tiny heart beating made Laurel's eyes fill with tears. There really was a baby inside of her.

A real, live baby. Her baby.

Brett placed his hand on her shoulder. His touch sent shivers shooting through her. "You okay?"

With her heart lodged in her throat, Laurel couldn't speak, so she nodded instead. Brett, the baby—having both of them in her life…

The picture on the screen changed to a different view. She still found it hard to believe she was looking at their baby in her stomach. It was so unbelievable. A miracle to end all miracles.

"Look at the little arms." She blinked to see if what she thought she'd seen was still on the screen. It was, and she smiled. "Is Junior sucking its thumb?"

Brett laughed. "Looks like it."

She reached for his hand and squeezed once. He squeezed back. They might not be right for each other or love one another, but they would do the best they could to raise their baby. She knew that in her heart.

Rex motioned to the monitor. "Those two dark spots are the kidneys."

Kidneys. Laurel could barely contain her excitement. She'd never realized how fascinating internal organs could be.

"Okay," Rex announced. "If you don't want to know the sex, I suggest you close your eyes."

Her gaze met Brett's, but she couldn't read anything in his dark eyes. "What do you think?"

"It's up to you."

"It's up to us." Laurel knew he had as much to do with Junior being here as she did. They were giving each other the greatest gift—a child to love and raise. Decisions had to be made together.

He smiled. "Let's wait."

"You're the third couple today who didn't want to know." Rex pushed a button. "You're stealing my thunder."

"Sorry." Laurel covered her eyes with her hands. "No peeking."

Brett laughed. "Don't tell me you never tried to find out what you were getting for Christmas?"

She kept her eyes tightly closed. "Once. I found every single present. It was the worst Christmas of my life."

More buttons clicked. "You can open your eyes now," Rex said.

"Could you tell?" she asked.

Smiling, Rex nodded. "If you want to know…"

"I don't."

"You'll be able to find out from the amniocentesis report if you change your mind." Rex tore off a picture from the machine. "Here's a photo for the baby's scrapbook."

Laurel held it in her hands as if it were a newly discovered van Gogh. To her, it was as valuable. More so, actually. "Thank you."

Brett cleared his throat. "Could I have one, too?"

Rex pushed more buttons on the machine and another appeared. "You can put it on your desk."

Brett grinned. "My thought exactly."

"Your doctor will get a full report," Rex said, "but none of the markers for Down's syndrome showed up on the ultrasound."

"That's great," Laurel said.

Brett drew his brows together. "But you want to know for certain, right?"

She did, but if anything went wrong, she would lose not only Junior, but Brett, too. A heaviness set into her heart. Before seeing the baby, she'd been so sure about having the test done. Logically, she still wanted to know, but... She glanced at Brett. "Is that still okay with you?"

That afternoon, Brett peeked his head inside Laurel's room. After the amniocentesis, he'd taken her home and fixed lunch. Once she'd eaten, she'd disappeared upstairs to take a nap. That had been two hours ago, and Brett was concerned.

"Laurel?" he whispered.

"Come in." Her voice sounded so soft, almost fragile.

He stopped inside the doorway. Laurel lay on the bed, curled up on her left side. Her hair was spread out over the plum Egyptian cotton pillowcase. Her bare feet peeked out from the cotton-weave blanket covering her. Her vulnerability touched his heart, and he wanted to make everything better for her. If only he could...

"I brought you a few things." He carried a stack of clothing, his clothing: sweatpants, sweatshirts, dress shirts. Until he'd seen her belly at the ultrasound, he hadn't realized how big she was getting or how tight her clothes fit. Amazing what a large shirt could hide. He set the clothes on the dresser. "You can wear them around the house."

"Thanks. I thought about asking, but..."

"Next time ask."

Her eyes brightened. "I will."

"Did you nap?"

She nodded. "I didn't sleep well last night."

He hadn't, either. Neither said a word for a minute, but the silence wasn't uncomfortable. "Can I get you anything?"

She started to speak, then stopped.

"What?" he asked.

"After everything that's happened today, would you mind...would you please hold me? Just for a minute."

That was something he'd do with pleasure. He smiled. "Do you want me to time it?"

She smiled shyly.

He climbed in bed and lay next to her. She scooted against him, her back to his chest, and he wrapped his arms around her. "How's this?"

"Perfect." She snuggled closer. "Thanks."

"Anytime." And he meant it. Brett buried his face in her hair and inhaled the minty scent of her shampoo. Now this was the way it should be. Every day and every night.

What was he thinking? They were going to marry because of the baby. No other reason. But as he held her in his arms, it was easy to forget reality, forget it wasn't only the two of them. That without Junior, she wouldn't be here.

"We made the right decision today by having the amnio, didn't we?"

Her "we" pleased him. It was time he made some headway. "Yes. We'd already discussed it."

"I know, but... I hadn't really considered the risks involved. I was only thinking about me and how badly I needed to know, even though knowing won't change anything." She struggled for each word, and Brett tightened his arms around her. "I'm feeling really selfish right now. A mother should put her child's needs first."

"You have put Junior first. You left your home, you got a job, you're learning to handle your own finances."

"I keep telling myself everything I'm doing is for the baby, but today I had the test only for me. Not Junior. Not you. If something happens because of the amnio—"

"It won't."

"You sound so certain."

"The risks of complications are low. You'll be fine."

"Everything always boils down to numbers for you. Must be nice."

"Many things do, but not everything." Laurel sure didn't.

"A baby certainly doesn't. Today I realized I know nothing about babies or kids. You'd think they'd come with instructions." She sighed. "I want to be a good mother, but what's going to happen once I have Junior and we're released from the hospital?"

"You'll get home and figure it out. Just like every other mother in the world does when she has her first child."

"It's a little scary to think about."

"It is."

"You don't know how good that makes me feel to hear you agree." Laurel cuddled even closer. She fit so perfectly against him. Like two halves that had become one. "Not that you're scared, but you have everything together all the time."

"Me? Hardly," he admitted. "Why do you think I have all those books? I've never changed a diaper before."

"Me, neither."

"Why don't we sign up for one of those baby care classes?"

"That would be great." Enthusiasm and relief filled her voice. "Would you mind if I read some of your books?"

"Not at all," he said. "We could read them out loud to each other, too."

"That would be nice. Just like this is." She put her arms on top of his. "I'm so happy you're the father of my baby. I couldn't imagine going through this with anyone else."

"Thanks, but what about your ex-fiancé?" He realized

what he'd asked. "I'm sorry. That's none of my business."

"It's okay," she said. "Charles and I—my ex-fiancé
was Charles Kingsley—"

"Kinsgley Enterprises?" Brett knew the successful
company well.

"Yes. Charles is the great-great-grandson of the first
Kingsley. We grew up together. From the time we were
little it was assumed we would marry and keep all that
money in the family, so to speak. Love never entered into
it. Charles wanted a trophy wife and I fit the bill. I'm sure
if I'd gotten pregnant I would be nothing more than a
trophy incubator."

That didn't sound like much of a marriage to Brett, yet
he realized he wasn't offering Laurel much more. But
their situation was different. A baby, *their baby,* was involved, he rationalized. "Why did you agree to marry
him?"

"I've asked myself that a million times," Laurel admitted. "Charles was handsome and rich, perfect husband
material, as my mother would say. Not the best reasons
in the world to get married, but it made sense then, and
we got engaged my senior year of college. Of course, I
never knew…"

"What?"

"How much I would have been missing had I married
Charles. We had lots in common, but we never advanced
past the kissing stage even once we were engaged. He
never pushed, and I always let him take the lead. It's kind
of strange now that I look back on it, but I guess since
we didn't love each other we didn't feel the need to…
That should have been a sign."

The guy must have had ice running through his veins

if the only thing he wanted to do was kiss Laurel. "I'd say so."

"I always dreamed how perfect my wedding would be, but the honeymoon... I never realized what all my friends meant when they spoke about the, uh, physical side of their relationships until you kissed me during the wedding ceremony. Suddenly it was so clear. I'd never felt anything like that before. It was better than all the fireworks on New Year's Eve 1999 combined. And I didn't want it to end."

Brett couldn't deny how much effect her words had on him. A satisfied smile formed on his lips. "Is that what you meant in your note about your expectations being exceeded?"

"Yes. You remembered that?"

"You could say it stuck with me."

"Everything stuck with me."

If only she would stick with him! Brett remembered undressing her. Undoing each of the pearl buttons on the back of her dress and pushing the gown off her shoulders, past her hips, down her legs. She'd stood by the bed wearing a lacy white bra, matching thong panties and garter belt with white silk stockings. He'd never been more aroused in his life. And if he weren't careful...

"Thank goodness I never married Charles Kingsley," she said, not a bit of regret in her voice. "The second best thing that ever happened to me was getting dumped by him."

Brett's curiosity got the better of him. "What was the best?"

"Marrying you in Reno." She sighed. "You gave me a night I'll never forget and you gave me a child. What more could a girl want?" Lacing her fingers with his, she placed them on her belly. "I'd do it again in a heartbeat."

It was as if his own heart stopped beating. Her words touched a part of him he hadn't known existed. "So would I."

And it was true. He wouldn't give up what he had now for anything. He had to show her....

"That's really nice to know." She gave his hand a gentle squeeze, and he couldn't believe how one simple, innocent touch could send his blood roaring through his veins. "What I can't understand is why you're still single? After all, you're—"

"Handsome and rich?"

"Modest, too." He heard the smile in her voice. "How old are you, anyway?"

"Thirty-three."

"I can't believe I didn't know that. Still, I find it hard to believe you've made it this far without a band of gold on your finger."

"You make thirty-three sound so old."

"You know what I mean."

"I married you."

"A one-night marriage." She laughed. "That's what I call a lasting commitment."

Just give me the chance. The thought shocked him. After all, this wasn't supposed to be a love match. They were marrying for Junior's sake. No other reason, he reminded himself. "There have been a few women in my life, but the majority of my time these past few years has been spent building MGI."

"Brett Matthews, don't tell me you've been living the life of a monk."

"No, but..." This was a touchy subject for him. One he didn't share with anyone. But it was becoming clear Laurel Worthington wasn't just anyone. A point he wasn't ready to contemplate too much. If ever. "The ones I wanted to get serious with didn't want to get serious with me.''

''The women you dated don't sound very smart to me.''

''Thanks, but most preferred someone like Henry Davenport, who was old money and offered them a way into the exclusive clubs in Portland, rather than nouveau riche like me.''

''As if Henry will ever marry.''

''True, but it was a game to him. It wasn't to me.'' Brett thought of all the times he and Henry had butted heads, like two rams battling for space on a mountainside. Yet Henry had still been Brett's first account when he opened MGI. ''Hard to believe we were as close as brothers, but he was still my nemesis.''

''So it went beyond his father?''

''Way beyond.'' Disquieting memories made the past seem as if it were yesterday. ''We're the same age and grew up competing in everything—school, sports and as we got older, women. There was one, Miriam. She was old money like the Davenports. I had graduated college and was working for a local investment firm when we met. We started dating. Things were going so well. I thought she was the one, and I planned to ask her to marry me, but when she found out I was Henry's housekeeper's son…''

''You never got the chance to propose.''

''I didn't. She ended up going out with Henry a few times….''

''I'm sorry, Brett.'' He didn't know what he expected from Laurel, but her sincere tone was more than he'd hoped for. ''But I can safely say both Junior and I are happy you didn't marry Miriam. Otherwise, we wouldn't be here.''

A strange thought. He couldn't imagine Laurel being anywhere else but right here in his arms.

Just lying next to her sent Brett's temperature up. Way up. He smiled, unlaced his hand from hers and touched her hair.

"See, everything worked out the way it was supposed to," she continued. "If I hadn't lost all my money, I would have married Charles, and if you would have had money back then, you'd have married Miriam. Poor Junior here would be nonexistent! Just goes to show you, it must have been fate."

That was one way to look at it. As he combed his fingers through her hair, the soft strands flowed over his fingers like silk. "Must have been."

Laurel rolled over and faced him. "So what do you think fate has in store for us next?"

Brett knew what he wanted. He caressed her cheek. No woman had a right to be this gorgeous. "What do you want to happen?"

As if weighing the question, Laurel closed her eyes. "I want…"

She parted her lips, the only sign he needed. He leaned toward her and brushed his mouth against hers. At the sweet taste of her, he knew Laurel had been right. Fate had brought them together.

But Brett didn't want to push, so he backed away. As he outlined her lips with his fingertip, she stared up at him, her eyes full of desire, full of longing. He wanted to kiss her again and again. But only if she wanted that, too. He wasn't sure what to do next, but Laurel took care of that.

She moved toward him and kissed him back. Her lips moved over his, taking all he had to offer. Brett wanted to be gentle, tender, giving. But he wanted her so much, too much. His hunger took over, but Laurel didn't back away. She matched him step for step without any hesitation, without any question. He was spinning out of control, but there was nothing he could do about it.

As he kissed her neck, soaking up the scent and taste of her smooth skin, she moaned. The sensuous sound nearly pushed him over the edge. She kneaded his shoulders and back. The feel of her hands on his muscles…no way could he relax when all he wanted was for her to keep going and never stop. He'd longed for her to touch him like this, like she had in Reno. But he never thought it would feel as good as it had then. As she trailed kisses from his mouth to his ear and showered teasing nibbles on and around his earlobe, Brett thought he would explode. A few more minutes…

Who was he kidding? Another couple of seconds…

He pulled away. Laurel's flushed cheeks and swollen lips made him realize how out of hand things were getting, or would have gotten had he continued.

It would be so easy.

His heart pounded in his chest, and he struggled for a breath. He wanted to blame it on the situation, the high emotion of what had happened earlier today. He wanted to chalk up the way he felt to the physical nature of their kiss, though a kiss seemed like a weak definition of what they'd shared. He wanted to believe it was a once-in-a-lifetime-never-to-be-felt-again kind of moment.

It was all of those things and then some.

Everything he'd felt in Reno he'd felt again. But it had been better. Much more satisfying.

And it scared him to death.

Chapter Eight

On Saturday morning, Laurel sat on the nursery floor ready to get to work. She knew what she wanted to accomplish this weekend, but as she laid out the four-inch-high, wood alphabet letters, a heavy feeling settled in her chest. She shook it off and concentrated at the task at hand, double-checking the letter colors against those in the comforter and crib skirt. Tears clouded her vision.

Who was she kidding?

Her insides were tied up in knots. Over the two-week wait for the test results, over her kiss—make that kisses—yesterday with Brett.

There was nothing she could do about the wait ahead of her except have faith that everything would turn out for the best, but Brett...

The memory of what they'd shared was so vivid, she couldn't have forgotten it if she'd wanted to. Just thinking about those kisses made her lips tingle. But it went beyond that to the way he'd held her, comforted her, talked with her.

In that moment she could almost believe that what they'd shared in Reno, and what they were sharing yesterday, had been real. Something beyond physical attraction and chemistry. Something she was afraid to define.

He'd made her feel cherished and safe, loved and accepted. All those things, she told herself, she didn't need to feel. Or want to feel.

Yet she'd felt them.

And it worried her. No matter how much she might not want to rely on anyone but herself, Brett was becoming the other constant in her life besides Junior. He was the father of her child, so that wasn't too strange, but Laurel's growing feelings for him had more to do with Brett, the man, than Brett, the father.

If only she knew what to do about those feelings and him...

He entered the room. "Nice outfit."

At the sight of him, a shiver of awareness ran down her spine. Laurel ignored it and glanced down at the black-and-orange Oregon State University sweatshirt and the navy sweatpants she wore. Quite a difference compared to his choice of khakis and a blue, button-down oxford shirt, but she preferred sweats, a ponytail and bare feet when she wasn't working at MGI. Funny, she'd never worn sweats except for during P.E. Laurel never knew what she'd been missing. "It's quite comfortable, but I'm sure you already know that."

"Hey, they look better on you than me."

"Thanks, I think."

"If you get tired of wearing my clothes, I can always loan you the money to buy some new ones."

"I appreciate the offer, but these are fine." The last thing she could afford were impulse purchases she'd never wear enough to justify buying. Maybe one or two pieces if she found a good sale. Thank goodness she wasn't the same person she'd been. That person wouldn't have been a good mother for Junior. "Sarah's giving me some of her maternity clothes, and Debbie's checking with her sister-in-law to see if she has anything."

"Hand-me-downs?"

The distaste in his voice was clear and it surprised Laurel. He'd been in a similar situation when he was younger. Maybe not as bad, but…

"What if I charge you interest with the loan?"

"No, thanks." She couldn't believe how good it felt to say those words. "I'm happy to borrow whatever clothes I can."

He frowned. "You'd rather wear used clothes than buy new ones?"

"Beggars can't be choosers."

"You'll never be a beggar."

"Never say never." His tone irritated her. She'd never seen this side of Brett, and she didn't like it. He sounded so snooty, so snobbish. The Brett she knew was neither of those things. In that moment, Laurel realized she didn't know a lot about him. Whatever she might think she felt for him had no basis in reality. A twinge of disappointment shot through her, and she shook it off. It was better this way. "Don't forget, I'm on a budget."

He sat next to her. "Just remember, I want all new things for the house. No hand-me-down or used items."

"What about antiques? Remember that store we went to on the other side of the river? You liked several pieces in there."

"I thought we were just looking. I never realized you were going to buy used things for the house."

"I wouldn't exactly call the antiques we saw used.

They would fit the style of this house perfectly and were heirloom quality.''

"Buy new heirlooms."

"That seems like an oxymoron to me." Laurel didn't get it. "What's gotten into you?"

"You wouldn't understand."

"Try me."

"You grew up rich."

"Growing up rich doesn't mean you don't have any problems."

"Yeah, right. I used to climb trees and peek into the windows of the 'big house,' so I know how the better half lived." An edge of bitterness hardened his voice. "My mother did the best she could, but she was a housekeeper. We couldn't afford a lot of new clothes so she patched my pants and bought what she could at thrift stores and garage sales."

"At least you had clothes to wear."

"Sometimes I wished I hadn't. Imagine wearing something you considered 'new' only to find it was a neighbor's older brother's castoff."

Ouch. Her heart ached for Brett. She remembered teasing a classmate for buying an off-the-rack dress for a formal. It had never entered Laurel's mind that the girl could have been on a scholarship and might not have been able to afford anything else. "Kids can be…cruel."

"You have no idea."

She knew from her own experience how cruel adults could be, too. But Brett's pain was still alive inside of him, and he was hurting. Badly. Laurel struggled not to take him into her arms and wipe away all the bad memories—both his and hers.

His jaw tensed. "I was the outsider. I didn't belong, and everyone let me know it."

"But now you live here yourself. You do belong."
Brett's childhood had been difficult, but look how much
he'd achieved. Surely that erased many of the pains of his
past. She laid her hand on his, but only for a moment.
Any more... "You've come full circle."

"Exactly." His dark gaze met hers. "You may think
I'm being picky or eccentric or whatever, but I've worked
hard to get where I am and I want only brand-new things
for my house."

"Okay, but if you change your mind—"

"I promise you, I won't." Brett's decisive tone only
drove the point home. "I'm not the kind of man who
changes his mind, ever."

His words reaffirmed what she already knew in her
heart—it was futile to hope for anything more between
them. They may have come far, but they'd never reach
the end of the journey. At least not together.

"I don't remember seeing this pattern in the sample
books." He picked up the comforter. "Is this for the
crib?"

She nodded. The simple question brought everything
back to where it should be—with the baby. Junior was
what had brought them together and would keep them
together. Nothing more, she reminded herself.

"I found it hidden underneath a bunch of other ensem-
bles that were on sale." She noticed his surprise and her
confidence wavered. "It's okay if I buy new things on
sale, isn't it?"

"Sales are fine."

Thank goodness. Otherwise she'd never complete the
decorating scheme she'd planned underbudget.

He picked up a cranberry-red-painted *A* and motioned
to the rest of the letters. "What are these for?"

"See the blocks with letters in the fabric?" She placed

a French-blue-painted *D* next to the bedskirt. "I thought these would look better than a wallpaper border. I want to put a white chair rail on the top and bottom to define the alphabet."

"The color matches perfectly."

"I used craft paint." She saw the flash of concern in his eyes. "Nontoxic acrylic paint, so don't worry."

"What color will the walls be?"

"Ivory."

Brett smiled. "This will look great."

"I think so." Laurel actually knew so. She wasn't sure how, but she could sense it. Decorating came much easier to her than office work. She also found it more fulfilling. "We can fasten the letters to the wall with Velcro, so we can play with them and spell words once the baby is old enough."

"You've thought everything out, haven't you?"

She shrugged. "The baby won't have a room like this when I get an apartment, so I'd like to make the nursery here special."

His gaze caught hers, and Laurel swallowed the quarter-size lump in her throat. *Remember, it means nothing.*

"You're more than welcome to stay here as long as you want."

Laurel felt a twinge in her stomach. More like the flapping of butterfly wings or tiny bubbles being set loose. She thought it must be Brett and his offer, which she could never accept, but then it happened again.

The baby. That's the only thing it could be.

Brett leaned toward her. "Is something wrong?"

She touched her belly. "I think the baby moved."

"Are you sure?"

"I think so. Tell me what you think?" She placed his hand on her stomach, happy to share this moment with him. Times such as this were meant for both parents. Of course, once she moved out it would be much harder to share such milestones. She tried to ignore the guilt creeping up her spine. Another flutter. "Did you feel that?"

"No. Isn't it a little early for you to—"

"It has to be Junior." She repositioned his hand. "What about that?"

"No. Your stomach's so hard. I thought it would be…softer."

She moved his hand again. "Anything?"

"Sorry."

"Maybe it's too soon for you to feel it, but something is going on in there."

"I'll trust you on this one." He removed his hand from her stomach, and she missed the warmth of his touch. "There are some things only a mother can know."

"My father used to say…" Her voice faltered.

"You okay?"

She nodded, but thinking about her father brought back so many painful memories of what he'd done and how much he'd hurt her. And her mother… Laurel finally realized the enormous gap between her and her parents. A gap she knew would never be bridged. "What do I tell the baby about my parents? How do I explain to Junior that Grandfather and Grandmother Worthington want nothing to do with us?"

Brett's easy smile relieved some of her heartache. "You won't have to deal with that for a long time."

"But one day I'll have to tell the baby the truth."

"Maybe by then you and your mother will have resolved—"

"My mother wants nothing to do with us." The words were out of Laurel's mouth before she could stop them.

"She's your mother."

Not any longer. Brett deserved to hear the entire truth about Serena Worthington. Laurel wet her lips. ''Before my mother used the last of her frequent flier miles to fly to France, she asked me to call her 'Serena,' instead of 'Mom.' She felt being the mother of a twenty-three-year-old pregnant daughter would interfere with her ability to snare a rich husband. Her words, not mine.

''I know she went through a lot with my father, but you'd think the one thing she'd want to hang on to was her daughter and grandchild.''

''Come here.'' Brett pulled her close, and she buried her head against his chest. He was so strong. So much stronger than she was, and Laurel relished the moment of security she felt being in his arms. ''Your mother doesn't know what she's losing.''

''Even if she does, she doesn't care.'' The truth hurt Laurel more than she wanted to admit. Her heart seemed to shatter into a million pieces. She couldn't understand her mother. Not then, and especially not now when Laurel was going to be a mother herself.

But she couldn't forget the lesson she'd learned. And one she needed to put into action. She might want to be close to Brett and gather strength from him, but she couldn't.

Not now, not ever.

He'd made both his intentions and his feelings clear— he only wanted to marry for Junior's sake, to give their child a family. Laurel appreciated his honesty, and she, too, desired to give Junior a family, but she could never marry for any other reason but love. She knew that in her heart and in her soul.

Using an enormous amount of willpower, she backed out of Brett's comforting embrace. ''I'll never be like my mother. Never.''

* * *

What a day to top off an already rocky two weeks. As Brett walked to the front door, he undid his necktie. The market had opened up, dropped after lunch and continued a downward spiral until the closing bell. It had taken too many phone calls to calm a few high-strung investors. But that was part of the job even if it meant working until seven.

Thank goodness Debbie had driven Laurel home. She didn't need to put in long hours, though he knew she would if asked. Her willingness to work hard whether on the house or at the job continually surprised him. One would never guess she'd been a pampered heiress for her entire life. He respected her determination to succeed, even though she was doing much better at decorating the house than working at MGI. But no matter what she was doing, she gave it her all.

No doubt she'd taken her anxiety over the wait for the test results and turned it into something more productive than worry. That's what Brett had done these past two weeks, but it hadn't worked as well this time as in the past.

Work had always been his sanctuary, the place where he could lose himself and forget about everything else in the world... At least it had been until Laurel Worthington stepped into his life. Now even work was just another place to see her, to think about her, to want her.

She'd gotten under his skin; she'd invaded his dreams. The feelings made little sense. Brett wanted her to be a part of his life, but under his rules. No one else's.

Before he could unlock the front door, it opened.

Laurel smiled. "Long day?"

"One of the longest." But seeing her made it better.

He noticed her black jumper and how good, beautiful, she looked. "New outfit?"

"Yes, I found it on sale when I went out to lunch with Sarah yesterday. I never thought I'd be able to afford anything new, but I could and it's all thanks to you and the budget you helped me set up and stick to."

Brett gave a bow. "Mr. Budget at your service."

She chuckled. "You should write a book for people like me."

"Like you?"

"People who don't have a clue about money."

"You're no longer clueless."

"That's only because I have a good teacher." She smoothed her hands over her protruding stomach. "Look. Can you see how much Junior is growing?"

Daily, he noticed the subtle changes in her body. Her tummy becoming round, her breasts fuller. Her hair seemed thicker, shinier. Somehow the mother-to-be was turning into the sexiest woman he'd ever seen. After the last kiss they'd shared, he'd been afraid what might happen if he kissed her again, so he'd tried to keep his distance. Easier said than done, he was discovering with each passing day. "You're finally looking pregnant."

"I'll take that as a compliment."

"It was meant as one." He closed the door and set his laptop case in the foyer. The smells of basil, garlic and oregano lingered in the air. "Did you cook?"

Laurel pursed her lips. "You're going to ruin one of my surprises. Close your eyes." She took his hand. "Follow me."

Brett did as told, enjoying the feel of her soft skin over his. He missed touching her, being close to her. She stopped, and he ran into her back. The familiar minty scent filled his nostrils. Man, how he loved the smell of her hair. He wanted to feel the silky strands over his face. Over his chest. Over him.

He wanted her. Period.

He'd better be careful and stay away from her. Far away. He had to let her come to him. So far she hadn't. If anything, she'd kept her distance. But Laurel would, once she realized she was making it on her own. All the rest would come later. Much later, he realized with regret.

"This way." She led him a few steps to the left. "Okay, open your eyes."

Brett opened his eyes. "What..."

The dining room looked like something out of a magazine or from Martha Stewart, with an oval cherry table, splat-back Chippendale chairs, a server and china cabinet with buffet. Botanical prints, candlesticks of varying heights, rich gold-and-red draperies and fresh flowers completed the luxurious room. He found it hard to believe this was his house.

He walked to the table. It had been set with his grandmother's china, but those were the only pieces he recognized. The gold chargers, damask place mats and crystal goblets and glasses he hadn't seen before. "Am I in the wrong house?"

"If you are, so am I." Anticipation filled her eyes. "Do you like it?"

"I love it." He'd wanted to have a home where he felt comfortable, yet could entertain. Laurel had achieved both goals. "You did an incredible job."

"Thanks, but I did have some help pulling it all together, especially tonight." Still, she blushed at his compliment. "Sit down or your dinner will get cold."

"You really cooked yourself?"

She nodded. "But with everything that happened today,

dinner's more of an afterthought. I hope you don't have your sights set on a seven course meal.''

''Whatever you made will be fine.''

''I'll be right back.''

The salad was on the table. Brett sat and picked up a sterling silver fork. Laurel had done a wonderful job with the decorating, turning an empty room into something elegant yet warm.

She carried in two steaming plates of spaghetti with meat sauce. A basket of garlic bread was tucked under her arm. After she placed everything on the table, she sat. ''Dinner is served.''

A bottle of sparkling cider sat on the table, and Brett filled the wineglasses. Leave it to Laurel to think of everything to make this dinner so special.

''A toast.'' He raised his glass. ''To making a house a home.''

She tapped her glass against his, and at the clink, a high-pitched note hung in the air. ''Here, here.'' Laurel took a sip, then raised her glass again. ''I'd like to make another toast—to a healthy baby.''

''I'll second that.'' He lifted the glass to his lips.

''Wait,'' she said. ''You don't understand. The test results came back today. Junior's fine. Our baby is healthy.''

He nearly dropped his glass. ''Everything's okay?''

Eyes sparkling, she nodded. Brett never thought he'd feel so relieved as he did at that moment. He rose from his chair and walked to Laurel's side. ''When we hadn't heard anything, I thought something must be wrong.''

''Nothing's wrong.''

Brett bent down and wrapped his arms around her. Damn, she felt so good against him. As if she belonged there. Always. She hugged him, and a piece of his heart melted. Much too soon she let go of him, and he felt an odd emptiness. Not only in his arms, but in his heart. Don't read too much into it, he told himself. This was about Junior, nothing else.

Brett couldn't believe how happy he was, happier than he'd ever been. It was more than relief. The weight of the last two weeks had finally lifted. For him and for Laurel. He saw it in her wide, perfect smile; he saw it in the twinkling blue of her eyes.

"I wanted to tell you at work, but Debbie said you were having a rough day so I thought it would be better to wait."

"If I'd found out at work, I would have been useless the rest of the day." The way he would be tonight. As soon as dinner was over, he wanted to celebrate. Dessert and dancing. He would spin Laurel around the room until their feet could no longer take it. Then he would lower her into a dip and kiss...

"I'm glad I waited."

"Me, too." But Brett wasn't satisfied with waiting for her any longer. She needed a little shove, something to speed up the process. A project to show her all she could accomplish on her own. A way to let her shine both at MGI and at home. And then it hit him. A way to do it all. "Laurel, what do you think of a party for our premium clients?"

Her eyes lit up even more. "Great idea. I'm sure there are some elegant places here in Portland—"

"I was thinking of having it here. Would you be interested in planning the party and being the hostess?"

Her features changed. She looked startled, like a deer caught in the headlights. "But the house isn't ready. The living room furniture is still on order and Renée isn't sure when things will arrive. The bookcases for the library aren't supposed to be installed for two weeks and—''

"Have Renée pull some strings and bump up delivery dates. Get done what you can before the party and wait on the rest,'' he said. "It'll take you at least a month or two to pull the party together. Think you can handle it?''

"Yes.'' There wasn't the slightest doubt in her voice.

"I'll give you a head count and a budget. On Monday you can check my calendar with Debbie and pick a date. Everything else is up to you. Since this is for MGI clients, we can lighten some of your regular workload so you can devote the majority of your efforts to planning the party.''

"I don't want any special treatment.''

"You're not getting any. Trust me. Just make sure whatever you do appeals to our premium investors. Their backgrounds are varied—everything from a retired airline mechanic to Henry Davenport. But they all have very large accounts with us.''

She clapped her hands together and grinned. "This is going to be fun.''

Seeing her this excited pleased Brett. It wasn't only moving her one step closer to marriage; it was her enthusiasm, her genuine happiness at being given her own project. "Why don't you jot down some ideas and we can talk about it in a few days. I don't want to wait too long for the party, but I don't want to overwhelm you, either. Hire all the help you need so you don't overtax yourself.''

"Don't worry, I'll be fine.''

"I have complete confidence in you.''

"You don't know how happy I am to hear you say that.''

This would be a big step for Laurel. "You're turning our house into a home, and I know our party will be the talk of the town,'' he stated.

Her smile widened. "Go ahead, put more pressure on me."

He laughed. "I'm here to help you in any way I can. All you have to do is ask."

"I will."

The tone of her voice told him she would. He sensed this party would lead to a change, a very welcome change, in their relationship. *Mr. and Mrs. Brett Matthews.* He smiled at the thought. "We're in this together, Laurel. Never forget that."

Her gaze met his. "I won't."

Brett realized he never would, either.

Chapter Nine

"I have something…" The words died on Brett's lip. He stood in the doorway of Laurel's room and stared. Her wet hair was a mass of waves, and she wore one of his dress shirts. He was used to seeing her wearing one with a pair of leggings or sweats, but nothing covered her long legs now. Nothing at all. To make matters worse, not all the buttons were buttoned, either. He cleared his throat. "I'm sorry for… The door was open."

"It's okay, I just got out of the shower and was about to dress for the party." Her pink tongue darted out to moisten her lips, and Brett's groin tightened. "Can you believe it's tonight?"

"No." He forced the words from his dry throat. After nearly two months of planning, the day of the party had arrived. But imagining what Laurel wore, or wasn't wearing, under his shirt was enough to make Brett forget everything.

"Did you need something?"

Oh, yes. He needed something, all right.

He needed…her.

Brett sighed. He'd held it together all this time and kept his distance, afraid he might push too hard, afraid he might blow whatever chance he had with her. This was her time. A means to an end for both of them. But now, when she was so close, when she looked so sexy, when he could smell the scent of her soap, her shampoo, her…

Get control, Matthews.

Brett struggled to stop the pounding of his heart, the racing of his pulse, the boiling of his blood. *Remember why you're here.*

He reached for the large white box, tied with a yellow satin ribbon, he'd stashed outside the door, and gave it to her. "This is for you."

She took the present in her hands. "You didn't have to—"

"I wanted to." Eager to see her reaction, he motioned to the box. "Aren't you going to open it?"

"If you're going to twist my arm…" She set the box on the bed, untied the ribbon and raised the lid. "I wonder what it could be…" She pulled back the tissue paper, and a small gasp escaped her lips. "Oh, Brett." The smile on her face was worth the price of the dress and then some. She touched the shimmering fabric with her fingertips. "It's the most beautiful dress I've ever seen."

"I thought it would look good on you." Okay, that wasn't the entire truth. He'd been having lunch in downtown Portland when he saw the midnight-blue dress in the window of an upscale maternity boutique. Long sleeved with a scooped neck, the dress didn't have any elaborate detail or stitching, but looked as if it had been made for Laurel. Brett had purchased it on the spot without any hesitation. "I know you want to buy your own clothes, but tonight's a special occasion and you've earned it for all your hard work.''

She lifted the dress by the shoulders. ''I did earn it, didn't I?''

''You did.'' He grinned, happy she hadn't given his gift back to him. ''You not only got the party put together, but the house. And you still managed to get work done at the office.''

She blushed. ''You'd better be careful or I'll ask for a raise.''

''I'd better be careful or I'll give you one.''

Laurel's eyes glistened. ''Thank you so much.''

Her grateful look made his throat constrict. It took so little to make her happy. He couldn't wait until they were married, until he could give her so much more than just one dress. ''You're welcome.''

''I guess we'd better get busy or we'll be welcoming our guests dressed like this.''

Brett nodded, but he could think of worse things at the moment. Much worse.

Laurel practically floated down the stairs, feeling like a princess—a pregnant princess, but one nonetheless.

''You look stunning.'' Dressed in a black tuxedo, Brett greeted her at the bottom of the stairs with a dazzling smile. Gold specks she'd never noticed before danced in his brown eyes.

Laurel's breath caught in her throat. So handsome. So male. So Brett. ''You do, too.''

''Let me see the dress.''

She twirled and the skirt flared as she spun. ''What do you think?''

''You look better than the house does.''

''As long as I don't look as big as the house.''

Brett laughed. "You have a long way to go for that."

She peeked into the living room to make sure it was ready for the onslaught of guests. Everything was in order. Fresh flower arrangements filled the air with a light floral scent. Even the decorative throw pillows had been fluffed.

"Anything else you need to do?" he asked as they moved into the dining room.

She checked her pearl stud earrings. They were the only real jewelry she had left, and she didn't want to lose them. "I think that's…" She glanced at him. "No, wait. I need to straighten your bow tie and cummerbund."

As she moved toward him, he took off his jacket, his gaze meeting hers. "Everything looks wonderful. I feel as if I'm in a dream."

"Me, too." She stood directly in front of him, her hands on his waist.

For a moment, neither said a word. Times like this had happened over the past two months, but Brett hadn't touched her, hadn't kissed her since that afternoon of the amniocentesis. Logically, she knew it was for the best. But she couldn't deny the way another part—her heart, perhaps?—wanted one more kiss, one more taste of him. Forget about the lack of logic, forget about the lack of a future for them. That's what she wanted. Now more than ever.

He smiled, a charming toe-curling smile that made her feel all fluttery inside. She smiled back. Suddenly, her fingers wouldn't do as her brain commanded. She felt as if she were all-thumbs when she finished with the cummerbund and went to work on his tie.

"Is it straight yet?" he asked.

He was so close, only her pregnant belly kept them from getting any closer. "Almost."

She ignored the warmth emanating from him. Ignored

the beating of his heart when her arm touched his chest. Ignored his soap-and-water scent threatening to drive her wild. Laurel held her breath and finally got his bow tie straight. "All finished."

"I'm not."

Brett's lips touched hers. Everything she'd been holding in, pretending not to feel, came rushing to the surface. She'd wanted to believe that she didn't want him, that he hadn't mattered to her, that he was only the father of her child. But she did and he had and he was so much more than that.

He deepened the kiss and she followed, willing to go wherever he wanted to take her. There was no yesterday, no tomorrow. Only now. She leaned into him, and he pulled her close, as close as her tummy allowed. Heat pooled in her and made her want what she knew she couldn't have.

Brett drew the kiss to an end and smiled. "For luck."

For keeps. Every sense seemed to be heightened, every nerve ending tingled. Laurel struggled to regain her breath, to regain control. Her pulse rate slowed; her heart stopped pounding. If only she could control the situation as well...

The doorbell rang.

Brett's grin widened. "Perfect timing."

That was a matter of opinion. A mix of odd emotions ran through her. Disappointment, relief, confusion and regret.

He shrugged on his jacket and extended his arm. "Shall we go and welcome our guests to our not so humble abode?"

The party was going well, and Brett couldn't be happier. The guests were enjoying themselves. He was making an effort to speak to each one of them, to make sure they knew how much they counted to MGI, but along the way, he'd lost track of Laurel.

"Great party, Brett. Bet we see even more money pour in." Alex Niles patted him on the shoulder, then was off to schmooze with another client.

Leave it to the boy wonder. Brett chuckled and searched the crowd for one of their most important investors, Marvin Crenshaw. The elderly man had made his money in timber and real estate. He owned a ranch and a winery in the Willamette Valley and resorts in Bend and on the coast. He was also a royal pain in the butt, but his account balance more than made up for the sour attitude.

Brett caught sight of the tall, lean man wearing his trademark Stetson, and standing right at Mr. Crenshaw's side was Laurel. Brett's heart rate speeded up.

He thought he'd imagined she looked like a goddess earlier. He hadn't, and he struggled for a breath.

The way she'd pulled her hair up made her neck look even more graceful, like a ballerina's. Her only jewelry was a pair of pearl stud earrings. She didn't need anything else.

And the dress…he'd been right. It looked as if it had been made especially for her. The scooped neckline accentuated her full breasts. The flair of the skirt didn't hide her pregnant stomach, but complimented it. She was radiant, elegant. And so close to being his he could taste it. Just as he could still taste her sweet kiss.

Laurel said something to Mr. Crenshaw. His weather-beaten rough face crinkled into a smile, and he laughed. A real laugh. In the last five years, Brett hadn't known the old geezer was capable of even smiling. Growling, yes. Laughing, no.

Brett couldn't believe her ease at conversing with the

wealthy investor. Crotchety Mr. Crenshaw could make even the unflappable Alex Niles nervous, yet Laurel looked completely at ease, completely in her element. She was a real asset, Brett realized, and wasting her people and entertaining skills at MGI. Once they were married...

He walked over to them. "Good evening, Mr. Crenshaw."

"Matthews. Nice party. And those bookcases in the library. Might have to get me a few of them." Mr. Crenshaw turned his attention back to Laurel. "Don't forget what I told you, young lady."

"I won't, Marv."

Marv? She was calling him Marv? No one dared call Mr. Crenshaw by his first name, Marvin, let alone Marv.

Laurel merely smiled as if it were nothing. "Be sure to let me know how B.K. is doing."

Mr. Crenshaw nodded. "Speaking of which, I'd better get home. B.K. doesn't like me to stay out too late." Mr. Crenshaw nodded to Brett, then kissed Laurel's cheek. "Stay off your feet. You don't want those pretty ankles of yours to swell."

"I'll be careful," Laurel said. "Don't forget to call me."

"I won't. Good night." The grizzly old man tipped his hat and headed to the front door.

Brett couldn't believe what he'd just seen. That couldn't be the same Marvin Crenshaw who was always threatening to close his account. The Marvin Crenshaw who didn't like being put on hold and wanted his phone calls returned immediately.

"He's such a nice man," Laurel said.

"Nice?"

She nodded. "Did you know he has a cat named Big Kitty? Tomorrow Big Kitty, or B.K. as Marv calls him, is having surgery. Marv's really worried. You should send him flowers."

"The cat?"

She sighed. "No, Marv."

"Why would I want to do that?"

"For the same reason you threw this party. To show your premium clients how much they mean to MGI."

"And you think this would make a difference to Marvin Crenshaw?"

"A big difference." The sincere tone of her voice told Brett she was serious. "He has no one except his cat. He's nothing more than an old man who's lonely and looking for some attention. Make him feel special."

"But it's just a cat."

"Just a cat who's the sole heir to a billion dollar estate."

For the first time in a long while, Brett couldn't care less about Mr. Crenshaw's money, about anybody's money. All he could think about was Laurel. He tried to keep his breathing steady, but it wasn't easy. She was so close and smelled so good. She'd even worn her signature perfume tonight. Something she hadn't done since the day she arrived in Portland. He was surprised he'd noticed let alone remembered a detail like that.

She touched his arm. "If you don't order the flowers, I will."

At that moment, he would have done whatever she asked. The realization should have bothered him more than it did. "I'll send them."

She grinned. "Thanks."

Brett stared into her eyes. He wanted to steal a kiss; he wanted so much more than that. "You're really something."

Rising up on her toes, she whispered, "So are you."

* * *

Everyone seemed to be enjoying themselves. For the first time since starting work at MGI, Laurel felt as if she'd contributed something worthwhile to the bottom line.

And she couldn't believe all the compliments she was receiving. Not only on the party, but the house. A couple of guests even asked if they could speak with her about decorating their houses. But she didn't allow that to go to her head. Not when she had to explain she worked at MGI, but would pass their cards on to Renée, the interior designer who'd assisted Laurel. Still, it had been quite a thrill.

Across the solarium, Brett glanced her way, and their gazes met. Time stopped. The music from the string quartet faded. The conversations of the party goers ceased. Laurel no longer smelled the delicious food prepared by the world-class caterer.

It was only she and Brett.

In this moment she could revel in the thought of the two of them together. Forever.

Thanks to the child growing inside her, their futures were entwined, but she wanted more. She wanted Brett to be a part of *her* life, too. She wanted it all. The marriage, the husband, the family. Tonight had made her see what she already knew in her heart.

But it wasn't going to happen.

Laurel had been engaged once for the wrong reasons, and even married Brett as part of a prank. She couldn't do it again for anything but the right reason—love. She couldn't follow in the footsteps of her mother and grandmother. She wouldn't settle for anything less than the best for her and Junior.

Touching her belly, Laurel looked away from Brett. She

wanted to lose herself in the crowd of guests. Something that shouldn't be too hard to do.

"Aren't you looking radiant tonight?" Henry Davenport, wearing a tuxedo sans bow tie, touched her shoulder.

"Henry." She greeted him with a hug and a kiss. "When did you arrive?"

"A short time ago." Handsome with light brown hair and hazel green eyes, Henry oozed charm and charisma. "I prefer to be fashionably late."

"Brett told me you were spending a few months in Europe."

"It kept raining so I decided if I had to be wet and look at dreary gray skies all day, why not be at home?" He took a step back. "Let me look at you." His blatant appraisal made her blush. "I see you have a bun in the oven. Congratulations. When's the timer going off?"

Leave it to Henry not to mince words. "December 23."

"That won't do at all," Henry announced. "You must have this baby on Christmas Day. We must keep the holiday birthdays alive."

He spoke as if having this baby on December 25 were as simple as making dinner reservations. "Babies have their own sense of timing, so don't get your hopes up."

"What would this world be without high hopes?" Henry furrowed his brow. "You know, Halloween is around the corner. What would you and Brett think about a masquerade wedding? The possibilities are endless."

"I bet they are," she said. "Why don't you tell me about your trip?"

"No wedding?"

"No." She saw the concern in his eyes. "It's okay. Really."

Henry took a sip of his champagne. "I hear you're at MGI?"

She nodded, thankful Henry had let the subject of a wedding drop.

"And you actually like to…work?"

He said "work" as if it were a foul word. To someone in Henry's position it no doubt was. She'd felt the same way not too long ago. "Yes."

He raised an eyebrow.

"I…it's okay."

"It's Henry you're talking to." He gave her an encouraging smile. "Tell me the truth."

"I'm sure working at MGI will get better once I've been there longer." She hoped she sounded diplomatic and not whiny, but office work wasn't her forte. Or wasn't yet, she corrected herself. "I had fun putting together the party. And I loved decorating the house."

"You did all this?" Henry glanced around. "Forget the job and MGI. Why don't you be an interior designer instead?"

"Decorate houses?"

He nodded. "You obviously have the talent. This house was nothing more than a shell. You turned it into a home."

"I don't have any formal training."

"You have innate style and taste—two things that can't be taught."

"I'm going to have a baby. Who's going to hire me?"

"Me," he said. "Help me with that mausoleum of mine. It still reeks of my parents. I want something that shouts 'Henry.'"

"I couldn't." But as she said the words a part of her wanted to jump at the opportunity. To take a chance and do something she loved. She remembered the business cards she'd collected earlier….

"You could. You did an incredible job with this house.

Of course, mine is bigger and more outdated. You'd have your work cut out, but I promise to compensate you…highly.''

She hesitated. Renée had wanted to talk to her about joining her staff, but Laurel hadn't wanted to discuss it. She felt obligated to stay at MGI. Brett had done so much for her. She owed him her loyalty, didn't she?

"You don't have to give me an answer now, but think about it. You owe it to yourself to be happy."

"I will."

"You will what?" Brett stepped in between her and Henry.

"Think about using Henry as a first name if it's a boy," Henry said before Laurel could answer. "And Davenport would make a good middle name for either sex."

Laurel chuckled, thankful for Henry's quick thinking and humor. "Thought this out, have you?"

"It's only fitting for my godchild to be named after me."

"Godchild?" she and Brett asked at the same time.

"Who else would you ask to be the godfather? If it weren't for me, you two would have never…you know." He nudged Brett with his elbow and winked. "I should be rewarded for my highly refined matchmaking skills."

"What about the dice?" Brett asked.

"They were *my* dice."

Laurel had succeeded. He had succeeded.

This wasn't only a victory for MGI, but a personal victory for Brett Matthews, outsider extraordinaire. Yes, his clientele ran the gamut, but tonight he'd impressed even those old money Portlanders. There was no sweeter feeling.

Brett was more than pleased, not only with how the

party had turned out, but by Laurel. She had outdone herself and proved what she could accomplish on her own. This had to be enough to make her realize she'd succeeded and could now marry him.

He'd been patient. He'd taught her the skills she needed to learn. Now it was time for Brett to get what *he* wanted.

He found Laurel in the kitchen, where she was giving final instructions to the cleanup crew. As soon as she was finished, she leaned against the counter and tucked a strand of hair behind her ear. She had to be tired, but he'd never guess it from looking at her. She was completely unruffled, as if she'd just gotten ready for the party.

"Ready to call it quits?" he asked.

"Almost." She straightened. "There are a few things—"

"Come on, Miss Hostess-with-the-mostest." He took her hand and led her to the sofa. "Those things can wait."

"But I still need to—"

"Forget about it. If the cleanup crew doesn't get to it, the housekeeper will tomorrow."

"Leave a mess? I don't believe what I'm hearing." Laurel felt his forehead. "You don't have a temperature. Why are you acting so strange?"

"What do you mean?"

"You can't be the same man who organizes his *Wall Street Journal*s by date and has all his magazines alphabetized."

Brett laughed at her shocked expression. "Believe what you want, but right now you're sitting down and putting your feet up."

He removed her shoes and placed her hose-covered feet on his lap. Slowly, he rubbed them. Each toe, the arch, the ball of her foot. As he did, Laurel sank deeper and deeper into the sofa.

Her lids heavy, she wiggled her toes. "You're the master of foot rubs."

"You've earned the five star special. The evening went off without a hitch."

"Not quite," she admitted. "The string quartet arrived late and the fruit could have been fresher."

He chuckled. "I doubt anyone noticed those things."

"If I did, someone else did."

"The evening was a complete success." He ran his hand up her smooth calf. "Anything you aren't satisfied with, you can do differently next time."

She sat up. "Next time?"

Once they married, he wanted to do lots of entertaining. Laurel was a natural at it. "I was thinking of Christmas?"

"Sounds like fun, except I'll either be out to here—" she placed her hand in front of her stomach "—or have a baby to take care of."

Junior. Brett couldn't forget the big date in the not-so-distant future. "We'll have the party at the beginning of December."

Laurel hesitated. "I suppose."

"You don't sound as if you want to do it."

She stared at the blank television screen. "It's…a little strange."

"What's strange?"

"This. Us," she said. "At MGI, everyone knows we were married and are having a baby. They treat us…normally. Well, as normal as can be, given the situation. But tonight…the investors assumed we're a couple and treated us as one."

"Does that bother you?"

"Not bother, but it's getting harder for *me* not to think the same thing."

Yes. Brett fought the urge to pump his fist.

"I mean, we spend all of our time together. And we have kissed... Sometimes it feels like we are..."

"A couple?"

She nodded.

He had to go slow. *S-L-O-W*. This was the chance he'd been waiting for. Laurel had opened the door, but he needed to proceed carefully. "Is that so bad?"

"Yes...no...I don't know." She sighed. "When I'm around you, no. But then when I'm alone..."

"You don't ever have to be alone again."

She raised her chin.

"I know you want to be on your own, but you have to realize by now I'm the last person who'd ever try to take away your independence. Thanks to my mom, I know what women are capable of doing by themselves. You've already shown me what you can accomplish on your own."

He stared into her eyes and tried to figure out what she was thinking. All he could see were pools of blue any man would gladly drown in.

She bit her lip. "How far do you see this...us going?"

Us. All the way. Until death do us part. For all eternity. Brett swallowed. "As far as we both want to take it. I still believe Junior deserves a family. A mother and father who are married and live together."

"What about parents who love each other?"

Love? That wasn't part of the deal. He couldn't lie to her, not even to get what he wanted. They had come too far for that. But maybe not far enough for Laurel. "I care about you."

He waited for her to say something. She didn't. He sat staring, feeling as if he were waiting for Greenspan to change interest rates again. Only much more was riding on Laurel's next move.

"I…care about you, too," she said finally. "But I don't know if that's enough."

Brett wasn't about to give up. "Isn't that better than nothing?"

"I…" She looked away.

"Would you rather I lie and tell you what you want to hear?"

Her gaze snapped to his. "No."

"I didn't think so." He took her hand. "I might not love you, Laurel Worthington, but I care for you…deeply. More than I ever thought possible. Isn't that enough for you to at least give it…give us a try?"

Chapter Ten

Seventy-two hours of giving "us" a try was all it took to convince Laurel she'd made a mistake. A huge one. She didn't need to give them a try because she was already in love with Brett Matthews.

Somewhere over the past couple of months, she'd fallen for him and fallen hard. She'd had an inkling at the party. Maybe more than an inkling, but she hadn't wanted to admit it. To tell the truth, she'd ignored all the signs until today. Until this afternoon at MGI, when Brett walked out of his office, smiled at her and said he would miss having dinner with her tonight. That was all it took to send her pulse racing, her heart pounding and her stomach feeling as if it had been turned into a butterfly refuge.

She loved him.

It was as simple and as complicated as that. The realization not only worried her, it terrified her. Loving Brett gave him control over her. Over everything. And that was the last thing she wanted after what had happened with her parents.

Not even the sight of Henry Davenport looking as if he'd stepped from the pages of an L.L. Bean catalog as he stood on a stepladder, hanging curtains in the nursery, could make Laurel smile.

"How do they look?" Henry asked.

She studied the drapes. "Too much of the top ruffle is on the left side."

He went back to work. Not an easy task, considering the window was over six feet wide, but he didn't seem to mind.

Looking for something to do herself, she straightened the forest-green-painted *K* in between the white chair rails.

How could she have fallen in love with Brett Matthews? It went against everything she was working toward. What made it worse was he didn't love her. And wouldn't love her even though he wanted her to marry him. She shouldn't have allowed herself to fall for him.

But how could she not have fallen in love with him? her heart countered. He'd trusted her to decorate his entire house, relied on her to plan MGI's investor party, stood by her side and helped her learn to handle her own finances, held her and supported her through the good and bad times of her pregnancy. Loving him was as natural as breathing.

Yet Laurel questioned her own feelings. Were they real or not? She needed to know the answer, but was afraid of what she might learn. The truth often hurt and so far this was no exception. She finally realized what she'd been doing since arriving in Portland. She'd allowed Brett to take care of her.

She wasn't doing it on her own. Not by a long shot.

And that was painful to realize, to acknowledge.

"Are they straight?" Henry asked.

Laurel glanced up. "Too much on the right now."

He went back to work. She made sure all twenty-six of the letters were securely fastened on the wall.

Yes, she was working, budgeting her earnings and saving money, but under Brett's guidance and under his roof. She was relying on him for everything—from her job to his support.

And if she continued to allow it to happen...

She couldn't give up her dream of making it on her own. Both she and her mother had allowed her father to shelter them, control them. Her grandmother had done the same. That was the Worthington way. But with Brett it would be worse, because he wouldn't only have control over the money, he would have control over her heart.

Time to break the cycle. Time to take charge of her own life.

Not only for herself, but for her child, too.

Laurel knew this was the only way. She had to be sure of herself and her love for Brett. She had to know for certain that what she felt for him was more than a desire for security. That her love was something real they could build a foundation upon, a family upon.

And once she'd proved all of this, maybe Brett's caring for her would turn to loving her. Maybe he would see what they could have together.

Henry sighed. "What about now?"

She looked up. "They're perfect."

He climbed down and examined them himself. "I like the teddy bears."

"So do I." The simple rod and pocket drapes were adorable with stars, moons and teddy bears on them, and they coordinated with the bedding. "Thanks for all your help."

He folded up the stepladder and rested it on the floor. "So are you going to tell me the real reason you wanted me to come over tonight? Or did you only want me to hang the curtains?''

"I wanted to speak with you, too." She was determined to make this work. So much was at stake, she had to make it work. Brett was at his business dinner and this was her best chance. She couldn't hem and haw. Time to just do it. "Were you serious about hiring me to decorate your house?''

"Yes," Henry said, much to her relief. "Are you considering it?''

"Yes, I am." Her voice sounded so confident, she almost didn't recognize it as her own. She picked up the tiebacks and fastened the first one to the wall. "I spoke with Renée Bernard, the designer who helped us, and she wants to take me on as her assistant. I would still have medical benefits, and she doesn't have a problem with maternity leave. She offered to help me with the cost of tuition for design classes.''

"And if you presented me as a new client—"

"I haven't mentioned you to Renée yet," Laurel admitted. "I wanted to make sure she wanted me, not your business.''

Henry smiled. "You've come a long way.''

"I'm trying. I still have a lot further to go." But she would make it. Laurel had no doubt about that. She attached the other tieback to the wall. "I only wish I'd realized it sooner.''

"What does Brett think?''

"He, uh, doesn't know yet.''

Henry's smile faded. "He's not going to like it.''

"He might," Laurel countered, but in her heart she knew the truth. "Okay, he probably won't, but I don't see any other way. If I don't get out of here and MGI, we won't stand a chance at…''

"Love?"

Nodding, she touched her belly. Junior had brought them together, but it was up to her and Brett to keep them together. She had to do her part first. "I really believe we can be a family, but I need to be sure of a few things first."

"When you accept your position with Renée, get a copy of her contract for me and find out what kind of retainer she requires."

"Oh, Henry." Laurel blinked back the tears of joy. She threw her arms around his neck and gave him a big hug. "Thank you."

"That's what friends are for."

"You're a great friend." She felt renewed, confident. Nothing could stand in her way. Laurel took a step back. "Now all I have to do is find an apartment—"

"I have a two-bedroom guest house. It's small, but charming in its own Laura-Ashley-meets-Laura-Ingalls-Wilder kind of way, and would be perfect for you and the little one."

"I couldn't."

"You could and you should. You'd be right down the street from Brett. Think how convenient that would be once you have the baby."

It would be convenient. But Henry was already doing so much for her. She wouldn't gain her independence by leaving Brett's house, only to start relying on Henry. "I'd want to pay rent."

He grinned. "I'd expect you to pay rent."

Part of her wanted to jump at the offer. It would solve all of her problems—except one. Her money situation. Henry wasn't known for his frugal living. She could only imagine what his small guest house would cost her. "I appreciate the offer, but I'm sure the rent would wipe out my savings.''

Henry's forehead wrinkled. "I thought the ring would cover all your debts and leave you with a little nest egg.''

She stopped arranging the pleats in the curtains. "What are you talking about?

"Your wedding ring from Reno.''

"You mean the *Titanic*-sinking-iceberg of a cubic zirconium?''

"Oh, no." He leaned against the wall and rubbed his forehead. "Do you still have it?''

Henry's pained look and tone worried her. She had no idea why he wanted to see her wedding ring. "It's in my room.''

"Get it.''

She hurried to her room, removed the ring from the music box and returned to the nursery. "Here.''

He took the ring from her. "You, of all people, should be able to tell this isn't cz.''

She studied the ring—the clear color, the faceted cut, the heavy weight. But she didn't see any flaws. Of course, she didn't have a jeweler's loupe. "If it's not cz, what is it?''

"It's a diamond.''

Her mouth dropped open. "But that would mean it's worth…''

He nodded.

If she'd known about the ring back in April, her life would be so different. Laurel would be different. She wouldn't have had to sell everything she owned. She wouldn't have had to leave Chicago for Portland. She wouldn't have fallen in love with Brett.

Henry slipped the ring onto her finger. "Your reward for participating in the tacky wedding adventure.''

Laurel stared at the sparkling stone with disbelief. Light reflected off the cuts and danced on the walls and ceiling of the room. How could it be real? And how could it be hers? She felt as if she were dreaming. At any moment, the alarm would ring and she'd wake up. No diamond on her finger, only a cheesy bauble tucked away in her music box. "Does everyone get a reward like this?"

"Some get more than others."

But that didn't make sense. Henry had money to burn, but why would he spend so much...? "You knew I was broke."

"I knew."

Only one other person besides her parents... "Charles Kingsley told you."

Henry nodded.

Her rat of an ex-fiancé. She clenched her teeth. "He promised he wouldn't say a word."

"He lied. He called to tell me I should uninvite you to the April Fools' bash due to your financial and family situation." Henry frowned. "I only wish you would have told me yourself. I thought we were good enough friends."

"Oh, Henry, we were—are—but I thought if I was poor you wouldn't..." Ashamed, she looked down at the floor.

"I may be a snob, but I'm a loyal snob." With his fingertips, he raised her chin. "I'm here now, aren't I?"

"Yes, you are." The caring look in his eyes reassured her, made her see she shouldn't have judged Henry the way she had. "I was wrong."

"I forgive you." A glint of amusement flickered in his eyes. Leave it to Henry to get a kick out of this. "And now you have the ring you can afford whatever rent I charge you for the guest house."

"Oh, oh my." The ring was hers. She wouldn't have

to rely on Brett.... As the realization sank in, she covered her mouth with her hands. "I can do this, I can really do this, can't I?"

"Yes, you can."

And then reality hit. "I can't. I need to do this myself." She removed the ring and handed it to Henry. "If I accept the ring—"

"You earned it." Henry slipped the ring back on her finger. "Whoever would have rolled the dice would have won the ring."

"Whoever?" His sheepish grin told her the answer. Only Henry would fix his own adventure. "You rigged it."

He started to protest, then gave up. "The dice were loaded, but don't let foolish pride stand in the way of getting what you want and giving your baby a family. Everyone gets a reward for participating. The ring was yours."

If she got one, then so did... "What was Brett's reward?"

"You, of course."

The dinner with community leaders dragged on way too long. Brett was tired, but he still stopped at the store to pick up flowers for Laurel. Things were going well between them. He was going to make sure they got better. And fast. He realized he didn't have much time to convince her to marry him. Before Junior's birth, Brett wanted Laurel to have Matthews for a last name.

He entered the house and heard voices. As he stepped into the family room, he saw Laurel sitting on the couch next to Henry. The cozy sight sounded warning bells in Brett's head. His fist tightened around the fragile bouquet he held in his hand.

Don't read too much into it.

Brett ignored the way his collar threatened to strangle him. "Hi."

Laurel's warm smile did nothing to take away the chill he felt. "How was your dinner?"

Every one of his muscles tensed. "Long."

Henry rose. "That's my cue to leave. I'll speak with you tomorrow," he said to Laurel. To Brett, he said, "Good night" and left.

Brett waited until the door closed. "What was Henry doing here?"

"Helping me hang the drapes in the nursery. My balance has been a little off lately and I didn't want to climb on the ladder."

"I would have done it."

"I figured you'd be tired when you got home."

He was tired, but the last thing he wanted was Henry taking over in *his* own house. It was Brett's baby, Brett's nursery. He was the one who should be hanging the curtains. "How do they look?"

"Perfect. All that's missing is a crying baby."

"You mean a sleeping peacefully baby."

"Isn't that what I said?" She motioned to the flowers in his hand. "Are those for me?"

Brett handed them to her. "Yes."

"Thank you. They're lovely."

As she walked to the kitchen and pulled out a vase, he followed. "They reminded me a little of your perfume."

Laurel sniffed the colorful bouquet. "They do. How sweet of you."

He didn't notice any other bouquets. At least Henry hadn't come bearing gifts. Brett was thankful for that.

She filled the crystal vase with water and arranged the flowers. "I've been thinking about my job at MGI. We both know I'm not the greatest when it comes to office work.''

He leaned against the counter. ''You've been holding your own.''

''Yes, but I'm not getting anywhere.'' She bit her lip. ''I don't think I'll ever get beyond where I am so... I'm going to resign.''

''That's wonderful.'' This was it. Brett felt it. All his tension disappeared; all his muscles relaxed. Thank goodness he'd already purchased an engagement ring. If only he had it with him instead of upstairs in his safe. ''You're making the right decision.''

She wet her lips. ''You think so?''

''Yes.'' His support seemed to surprise her. How could she think he'd let his wife work? ''There's no reason for you to continue working.''

''But I'm going to keep working.''

He didn't understand. ''What?''

''I'm going to work for Renée. She wants me to be her assistant.''

He tried to comprehend what Laurel was saying, but it wasn't making sense. Why would she need to work once they married?

''I can take classes and learn—''

''What about the baby?''

''Oh, I'm not talking about starting classes next week,'' she explained. ''I won't go to school until the baby is old enough to be left alone for a few hours.''

Brett wanted to be supportive, but he thought she would prefer to stay home full-time with Junior. It's what he wanted her to do. ''You enjoy decorating that much?''

''I love it. And I think I could be really good at it.''

Her eyes sparkled with a confidence and passion he hadn't seen before, and Brett knew she had to do this. It might not be what he wanted, but Laurel wanted it. Marriage took compromise. At least that's what he'd read in a book somewhere. "You'll be great."

"Thanks." She smiled. "I also thought it might be a good idea if I moved out for a little while. See how things go with some distance between us."

He straightened. "We don't need any distance."

"I'm talking space, not miles." She rearranged one of the lilies in the arrangement so it was at the center of the vase. "Besides, I won't be far away, just down the street at Henry's."

At Henry's. Brett's defenses went up. "No way."

Laurel did a double take. "What did you say?"

His throat thickened, and he forced the words out. "I won't let you go."

She stared at him, her eyes wide. "Excuse me?"

"You're not living with Henry."

"I'm not planning to live with him. I'm going to rent his guest house," she explained, as if she were simply going to the store to buy a loaf of bread. "It's the perfect place, since I'll be working on his house."

"You're not working on Henry's house." Brett would make sure she enrolled in the best interior design program he could find. He'd do whatever it took. Laurel was *his.* No way he would let his old friend win this time around. "I can offer you whatever Henry did."

"You don't understand. This isn't about you or Henry."

"No, it's about you and Henry." With a sinking feeling in his heart, Brett finally understood. He'd already lost. Hell, he'd never stood a chance. No matter how she might pretend his past didn't matter, Laurel Worthington was no different than any of the other women he'd known. Money, make that old money, was all that mattered to her. "You finally realized what marrying a Davenport would give you." The words left a bitter taste in his mouth.

"Marrying Henry Davenport would be like living in Disneyland." She laughed. "It might be fun, but after a while you'd want a break from Fantasyland."

"With his money, you of all people wouldn't need a break."

She narrowed her eyes. "Okay, this isn't funny."

"I'm not joking." He crossed his arms over his chest. "The apple doesn't fall far from the tree, after all. I'm sure your mother will be thrilled with your latest catch."

"Unbelievable." She slapped her palms against the granite countertop and glared at him. "After everything we've been through, that's what you think of me? That's what you think this is about?"

"You're the one who's set her sights on Henry."

"I have not." She planted her hands on her hips. "I'm doing this for us. No other reason."

"Yeah, right." Brett couldn't believe a word she said. He'd known that once, but forgotten. She was good, too good. He had to give her credit for that. "I'm sure all of Henry's money—"

"Money isn't the most important thing—"

"Money is important." She was the last person to tell him it wasn't. She had come to him for a job, to earn money. She was the one leaving him for...

She was leaving him. He felt as if he were being devoured by a man-eating tiger. A tiger with the initials L.W.

"So you've implied, over and over again." Her eyes darkened. "You know, you can't take it with you."

"Your father did."

The color drained from her face. Her lower lip quivered. Staring at the flowers, she took a deep breath.

Brett hadn't meant to hurt her. Oh, hell, yes he had. He couldn't help himself, because she'd hurt him. He'd allowed himself to fall into her trap again. To trust her when she said she believed in him, in the two of them, in a family.

The silence increased the tension between them, pushed them further and further apart.

"You're jealous." He expected her to sound angry, but she wasn't. Her tone was sympathetic. Damn her. He didn't want her sympathy. He didn't need it. But that didn't stop her. "You're still that scared little boy with patches on his jeans who peeked in the window to see how the better half lived, never realizing he *was* the better half. Not the people inside the big house."

Her disappointment in him was unmistakable, but he didn't care what she thought.

Laurel frowned. "I feel sorry for you, Brett Matthews. You could have anything you want in the world, yet you only focus on what you can't have. Money, wealth—it isn't everything. Who you are is so much more important than your net worth. I started to believe...no, I *did* believe we had a chance to be a family, but I was wrong."

No, he'd been wrong. Utterly and completely wrong. And he was losing the most important thing in the world because of it—his child. Brett's stomach burned. He felt physically ill.

"You don't even love yourself. How could you ever love Junior or me?"

"I never said I loved you."

"No, you never did. How noble of you." She tilted her chin and stared into his eyes. "Well, I loved you, or at least thought I did."

She loves me. A part of him wanted to grab on to her and never let go, but that was only his foolish half. Brett knew better than to believe a word she said, especially a declaration of love. He looked at the flowers. It was easier than watching the lies roll off her tongue.

"But love isn't always enough." Her voice broke, but she continued on. "I'd rather live a life of poverty than let wealth define who I am. If I've learned one thing through this entire ordeal, it's that. And the last thing I will allow you to do is taint my baby with your misguided beliefs, the way my father did with me."

She removed a ring from her finger and handed it to him. "Here." It was the ring from their Reno wedding. "Did you know this is a real diamond?"

He stared at the rock-size jewel in his hand. "Why are you giving it to me?"

"Because you need the money much more than I do."

The door slammed.

One phone call, and Henry had come running. He hadn't said a word to Brett, simply helped Laurel with her bags. Even now, after all these years, Henry was coming out on top. Some friend he'd turned out to be.

Well, good riddance.

Still Brett couldn't shake the feelings churning within him—relief at having it over once and for all mixed with dread at what was in the future. No matter how he and Laurel had parted tonight, their lives would be entangled because of Junior. He wouldn't let her keep his child from him. Even if it took every dollar he had, he would be a part of Junior's life.

Brett walked to the front door. The click of the dead bolt sealed the finality of it all. Tomorrow he would change the locks, get a new security code. He glanced at the living room. Despite all the furnishings, he sensed an emptiness.

Brett reached for the light switch, and he froze. Touches of Laurel were everywhere, from the paintings on the wall to the pillows on the sofa. He loved what she'd done with the decorating, but he couldn't live with it now. The reminders of her time here would be too much. Maybe Renée would refer him to another decorator. Brett couldn't go back to the way it had been before. He wanted to live in a home, not a place where he stored his stuff.

No matter what he might think of her, Laurel had turned his house into a home with both her decorating and her presence. She might be gone, but that didn't mean he had to stop doing all the things he now enjoyed, like spending more time here than at the office, cooking dinner instead of eating in restaurants, and hanging out with nothing to do except read baby name and child care books.

Except now he would be doing all those things alone.

Climbing the stairs, he straightened a photograph of himself and his mother that Laurel had hung. At the top of the stairs, he picked up one of her slippers. She must have dropped it on her way out. He'd stick it in her room. The guest room, he corrected himself.

The door to the room was open, and he stepped inside.

Except for the stripped bed, he would never have known she'd been here these past few months. He walked to the open closet. Only empty hangers remained. He tossed the slipper on the floor.

She was gone.

Gone for good.

It hurt more than it should.

As he turned to leave, something on the dresser caught his eye. He moved closer. It was the music box he'd given to Laurel in Reno. Funny, he'd forgotten all about it. He'd seen her admiring it at the wedding chapel and had bought it for her—a wedding gift, so to speak. He couldn't believe she'd kept it all this time…and the wedding ring he'd placed in his shirt pocket, too. She'd left him two reminders of their folly in Reno, while she'd taken the most important one with her.

Junior.

Brett wound the music box. Holding it in his hands, he closed his eyes and pictured Laurel walking down the aisle to him. One day soon she'd be doing the same with Henry….

No, she wouldn't.

If she'd wanted to marry Henry, why had she come to Brett in the first place? And if she were only after money, why had she given him the ring?

Because Henry had enough money…. *No,* a voice shouted.

Oh, hell. Brett blinked open his eyes. He'd been wrong.

Laurel Worthington wasn't doing anything except following her heart and reaching for her dream.

She wanted to be a good mother, a role model for Junior. But most importantly, she wanted to do it on her own. The last thing she wanted to be was a carbon copy of her own mother. Laurel had shared those things with him, and he hadn't listened. Oh, he'd listened with his ears, but not with his heart.

No wonder she didn't want to marry him, then or now. He'd never given her the right reason to marry him. He'd offered her everything but himself.

Brett had been doing everything for the wrong reasons. Not only with Laurel and Junior, but his entire life. If he'd felt sick before, that was nothing compared to the twists and knots forming inside him now.

Laurel had even told him she loved him.

She loved him.

And he'd assumed she was lying, and had said nothing.

His foolishness weighed down on him, and Brett struggled for a breath. He'd been a fool. A damn jealous fool.

By clinging to the heartaches and so-called injustices of his past, he was missing out not only on the present, but the future. All he wanted was to be accepted and loved. Laurel had done both of these things without a regard to his past. And he'd thrown it back in her face.

Brett turned the knob on the bottom of the music box once again. As the nest with the two love doves spun around and the wedding march played, he sank to the floor.

The apple doesn't fall far from the tree.

His own words came back to haunt him. He'd accused Laurel of being like her mother, when he wasn't so different from his father.

Damn.

Brett had strived to be the polar opposite of the man who'd fathered him, yet he'd failed. Failed both Laurel and Junior in the worse sense of the word. A father wasn't only there to provide income, to buy things, to be a figurehead. A father was there to support, to nurture, to love. As was a mother.

Junior needed both a mother and a father. Laurel and he had been half-wrong, but together they were right. Together...

How could he have been so stupid?

He finally knew what he should have realized a long time ago: all the money in the would couldn't buy the most important thing—love. So how would he show Laurel he'd learned his lesson?

Chapter Eleven

For the first time in a long time, Brett didn't have a plan; he didn't have a strategy. He had only one thing, a desire to see Laurel. Tonight. He didn't care that it was late. Waiting until morning was unacceptable.

At the closed gates to the Davenport estate, he keyed in the security code he remembered from his youth. The gates opened, and Brett drove his car in. So many years of entering through these gates. So many years of wishing this was his home. All this time it had been. The above-the-garage apartment where he'd grown up was his home, the lush estate grounds and gardens his yard, but he'd been too obsessed with living in the "big house" to see how lucky he'd been to have all that he did.

The porch light illuminated the formal double-door entrance. He pressed the doorbell, and bells chimed. A middle-aged woman, the housekeeper, Brett assumed, opened the door.

"I'm here to see Laurel Worthington."

"Miss Worthington is asleep." She slammed the door in Brett's face.

Not the welcome he'd expected, but he wasn't about to give up. He rang the bell again. No answer. Again.

The door finally opened. "Evening, Brett," Frank, the Davenports' long-time chauffeur and handyman, said.

"You know why I'm here."

"I can't let you in."

"Let me talk to Henry."

"He's retired for the evening."

Brett wanted to force his way in, but he knew that wasn't the way to go about this. "Henry never closes his eyes before 1:00 a.m."

"I'm sorry, Brett." The sincerity in Frank's wrinkled face was clear. "I really am."

"I know you are." Frank had gotten old. Brett thought back to all the times they'd played catch or worked on cars together. But it hadn't been enough for a boy who wanted it all. Who'd wanted only someone like Mr. Davenport to pay attention to him. "Thanks."

"There's always the tree." Frank winked and closed the door.

Leave it to Frank. Guests always stayed in the east wing. Brett had forgotten, but he remembered climbing the oak tree. He wasn't ten years old anymore, but he could still climb.

To reach Laurel, he'd try anything.

She couldn't sleep.

Thanks to Henry, Laurel was staying in one of his guest suites. She had all the amenities, including the turn down service of a fine hotel. But every time Laurel closed her eyes, Junior moved, turning somersaults and cartwheels and back flips in her stomach. She wanted to blame her sleeplessness on the in utero gymnastic routine, but she couldn't. Not when thoughts of Brett were the only thing keeping her awake.

It was over.

Whether she wanted to work things out or not didn't matter, because she couldn't fix their problems alone. She wouldn't want to try. And if she left it up to Brett... He was too caught up in the past. Too concerned with money and net worth to see what was really important in life. It was so sad. Like her parents, Brett didn't know what he was missing out on.

Tears filled her eyes, but she blinked them away. Brett didn't deserve to have her cry over him.

Yet her heart was breaking—for her, for Brett, for their baby. The three of them would never be a real family.

But that was okay, she realized with a start. She would make her own family. Her and Junior. A party of two.

Touching her belly, Laurel felt an arm or a leg pass under her palm, and she marveled at the new life growing inside of her. "It's just you and me, little one. But we're going to make it. I promise you that."

And she knew they would.

She had succeeded. It was only after walking away from Brett that she knew she was different from her mother and grandmother. Laurel could have taken the easy way out, married well and secured a comfortable life for herself and Junior.

But she hadn't.

She'd left that behind the minute she'd called Henry...no, even before that—the second she gave Brett the wedding ring from Reno. It wasn't without a great cost, either. Not monetary, but to her heart.

Still she took pride in how far she'd come. She'd truly changed from a spoiled heiress, who was once satisfied to be engaged to a man she didn't love, to a single, working, soon-to-be-mom, who faced a rough road ahead of her.

Her new awareness comforted her. And in time, her heart would heal. In time…

A tap sounded at the window.

A raccoon or small animal? Laurel ignored it and tried counting sheep. Anything to shut off her brain and the jumble of thoughts racing through it.

Another tap.

Maybe if she were more comfortable she could sleep. She repositioned the pillow between her legs and the one under her stomach. Now to count backward from a thousand.

A third tap.

What was that? Laurel flicked on the light, crawled out of bed and drew back the curtain. Brett's face greeted her. Was she dreaming? "What…?"

"Open the window," he mouthed.

She unlatched and opened the window. "What on earth are you doing?"

"I was in the neighborhood—"

"Get inside." The brisk night air rushed in and she wrapped her arms around herself. She wore a flannel nightgown, but not even that kept the chill away. "Before you kill yourself."

"I'm perfectly safe out here." He climbed in the window, then closed it. "Used to do it all the time when I was a kid."

Stunned and puzzled at his appearance at the window, she studied him. He was still wearing his tailored suit. Armani or Brioni, she guessed. And he'd ripped one of the knees of his trousers. The least he could have done was put on jeans or sweats if he was going to be climbing trees. One part of her wanted to tell him to leave. She didn't want to hear why he was here, but the other… Curiosity won out. "Why didn't you come through the front door like normal people do?"

"I tried, but they wouldn't let me in."

She could imagine who "they" were. Henry had only the best of intentions, but he could go a bit overboard. Though she was the one who'd told him she never wanted to see Brett again.

"I had to see you."

He gazed into her eyes, and she felt a flutter in her stomach. It didn't change what had happened earlier, what she'd learned about Brett. Reliving the pain of what he'd said…she couldn't go through that again. She raised her chin. "You've seen me, now go."

"Please—"

"I can't do this." Ignoring the pleading tone of his voice was one of the hardest things she'd ever had to do. But she had no choice. She had to look out for herself and Junior. "Not now. Maybe not ever."

"I'm sorry for what I said to you." He walked toward her. "Please let me make it up to you."

As he took her hand, a shiver shot up her arm and down her spine. Laurel pulled away. She didn't need him to start touching her and making her senses go haywire. Shivers or no shivers. "It's too late."

His eyes were full of regret. "It can't be too late."

Laurel said nothing. She was too confused by the mix of emotions running through her.

"The things I accused you of… I was wrong. You tried to tell me the truth, but I didn't listen. I didn't hear a word you said. My brain shut off and my heart took over. I'm not very good when it comes to dealing with emotions, as you found out tonight. But what I do know is I don't want to lose you. I can't lose you, Laurel."

The anguish in his voice clawed at her, but she had to keep her heart immune. "Lose me? You never had me." Even as she said the words she knew they weren't completely true. "And for your information, I don't need you."

"I know you don't," he admitted. "You're capable of taking care of yourself. You always have been, even before you arrived in Portland. You could have taken the easy way out when your father lost all your money. You could have married the first guy who stepped into your life. But you didn't. You picked yourself up and kept going. You didn't wallow in what had happened, but made a fresh start for you and the baby. Whereas I…my whole life I wanted to be like Henry. Hell, I wanted to be Henry. Pretty pathetic. But I've done a lot of growing up in the past couple of hours."

A glimmer of hope took root in her heart. "Brett—"

"Let me finish," he said. "I know you don't need me, but what I've come to realize is, I need you."

Time stopped. Everything stopped, including Junior. The only sound Laurel heard was the beating of her heart. No one had ever needed her. She forced herself to breathe.

Brett reached out and touched her hand again. "I need you, Laurel. I really do."

This time, she didn't pull away. She didn't want to. Hope grew into a bud, a fragile rosebud waiting for the opportunity to bloom.

"I thought I was the expert, teaching you about money, but it was the other way around. You taught me money isn't all that important. I didn't know I let the way I felt color what I did or thought. It tainted my view of everything, including you.

"When you first arrived at my office and I said I wanted to marry you, the only thing that mattered was the baby. I didn't want to be like my father. I didn't want my baby to grow up hating me the way I hated him. That was the only thing I could see and why I pushed for it so hard. But as we started spending time together, I realized this wasn't only about Junior, and it scared me. I thought you would never want me. I guess I'm still that little boy trying to prove his worth to everyone. I was afraid I couldn't prove it to you, so I ignored how I felt.''

Tears welled in her eyes. ''Oh, Brett. None of that matters to me. Not now, not in the future.''

''I know.'' He kissed her hand. ''That's one of the reasons why I love you so much.''

Her heart pounded in her throat. She couldn't believe this was happening. It was more than she could have imagined, more than she could have dreamed. ''You…love me?''

''I do, and I want to marry you. Not because it's the right thing to do or because Junior needs a father, but because I love you. It doesn't take a baby to make a family. We're a family right now.''

A family. Her own family. She swallowed…hard. Hope blossomed into a beautiful rose, an eternal bloom that would never wither and die.

''I'm far from perfect, but I'll do my best to be a good husband and father.'' His smile was earnest. ''I trust you with my heart, with everything I have. I don't want any prenups or agreements. I want you to be my equal partner whether we're in bed or doing business. You won't ever have to worry about not having money of your own. It's yours. No strings attached. I won't question what you do with it, whether you choose to spend it, give it away or save it. Hell, you can burn it if you want.''

Laurel knew how big a step Brett had taken, and her heart filled with joy. He finally understood that money wasn't everything. She wanted to laugh; she wanted to cry. She smiled instead.

"But you still have to rely on me."

"What?" she asked.

"Just like I have to rely on you. That's what being in love is all about. Being there for one another."

"I'm beginning to understand that." And so much more.

"I do love you, Laurel Worthington."

"I love you, too." There, she'd said it plainly. And she knew that she meant it. That the love she felt for Brett was real. One hundred percent real. There was no mistaking what her heart was telling her. "You're more than I ever hoped for in a husband or for the father of my child. You've helped me to reach my goals, you're giving me all I could ever ask for. I thought what we shared in Reno was magical, but this goes beyond magic."

Brett flashed her a devastating smile and kissed each one of her fingers. "Way beyond."

"I want to be with you, but I need some time on my own to prove I can do it myself."

"You don't need to prove anything to me."

"I know, but I need to prove it to myself," she admitted. "It was so easy to pretend I was making it on my own when I lived with you. You were always so supportive and caring. I felt so safe and secure with you around. I know that's the way it should be when two people love each other, but I need to follow through with what I planned on doing when I first arrived in Portland. Do you understand?"

"I understand." His eyes shone with love, and Laurel soaked it up. "Take all the time you need."

"I will." She knew she could love him and be her own person, too. She'd never felt so empowered. "But I'm giving you fair warning…you'd better be prepared to marry me once I'm ready.''

His eyes widened. ''Are you, Laurel Worthington, proposing to me?''

''I…'' *Worthington women always survive.* But Laurel was going to do much better than survive. She was going to take control. Wondering if Grandmama was rolling in her grave, Laurel raised her chin. ''Yes, I am. Isn't that what independent women of the new millennium do?''

''You tell me.''

Her gaze met his. ''Will you marry me, Brett Matthews?''

He smiled. ''I will.''

''Uh oh.''

''What?''

''I wasn't prepared for proposing, so I don't have a ring to give you.''

''That's okay.'' He pulled the diamond ring she'd worn in Reno from his shirt pocket. ''I hope this will do for now. The ring I bought is back at our house.''

Our house. Those two words were music to her ears. She extended her left hand. ''I love you.''

''And I love you.'' He slipped the ring on her finger. His lips touched her, and she felt something better than magic, better than anything else in the world—love. The baby kicked. Hard. Brett laughed. ''Do you think Junior's trying to tell us something?''

Epilogue

"**M**erry Christmas, darling." Brett leaned over and kissed Laurel's forehead. "I love you."

Her heart swelled with joy. "I love you, too."

Holding their daughter in his arms, he kissed her tiny, knitted-cap-covered head and caressed her cheek with his fingertip. "Merry Christmas, my little Noelle."

Laurel smiled at the sight. She'd never been happier or felt more content. She had a wonderful husband and a perfect, healthy baby. It didn't get much better than that. She only wished she wasn't so sore, but some sacrifices had to be made for the birth of her baby daughter in the wee hours of Christmas morning. Seeing Noelle cradled in Brett's arms made the discomfort worthwhile.

His eyes were full of love and life. "She's almost asleep."

"She's had a busy day."

"So have you." He lay the baby in the bassinet, picked up the music box and turned the small knob. The wedding march played. "This will lull her to sleep."

Laurel wondered why Brett had been so insistent the music box be packed in her hospital bag. Now she knew. "But the wedding march? Wouldn't 'Brahms's Lullaby' be more appropriate?"

His affectionate smile filled her with a warm glow. "Noelle will never know the difference."

The door to her hospital room opened and Laurel heard bells, what sounded like jingle bells, to be exact.

"Ho, ho, ho, Merry Christmas," a cheery voice called out. Santa Claus complete with velvet red suit, black leather belt, boots and white beard entered the room with a cloth sack swung over his back. "I was checking my list and saw I missed a brand-new baby girl who hasn't had the chance to be anything but nice."

As soon as Santa saw the baby, the bag on his shoulder fell to the ground. He froze, jingle bells included. "Is that her?"

Laurel nodded. "Would you like to hold your goddaughter, Uncle Henry?"

Wide-eyed, Henry stared at Noelle. "I don't want to wake her."

"It's okay," Brett said.

Henry removed his fake beard and picked up Noelle as if she were a fragile Fabergé egg.

"Make sure you support her head," Brett said.

"You don't need to tell me what to do." Henry rubbed his fingertip along Noelle's chin. "I took a class on caring for newborns."

Laurel exchanged a surprised look with Brett.

"Someone has to baby-sit her, and you'll leave her with strangers over my dead body." Henry rocked Noelle in his arms. "You're the most beautiful baby in the entire world."

Brett smiled. "She takes after her mother."

"She does. Your mommy and daddy did well, my little princess." Henry grinned. "They did so well."

Happy to have her family together, Laurel sighed.

Henry made a coochie-coochie-coo sound. "You're going to have so much fun with your uncle Henry. I'll put Auntie Mame to shame. Wait until your first trip to New York. We can go shopping at Tiffany's and FAO Schwartz and stop in at the Russian Tea Room."

Brett's forehead wrinkled. "Let's not—"

Laurel squeezed his hand. Now wasn't the time for him to be a protective father. "Noelle is lucky to have someone like you in her life, Henry."

For a moment, Laurel thought she saw tears glimmer in Henry's eyes, but then he blinked and they disappeared.

"Noelle." His smile widened. "What a perfect name for a Christmas baby. I told your mommy you had to be born on December 25, and I was right. Uncle Henry is always right."

"Uncle Henry is sometimes right," Brett corrected with a grin.

"We'll discuss this later." Henry lay Noelle back in her bassinet. "Santa asked me to do him a favor. He was a little busy last night."

From his sack, he pulled out brightly wrapped packages with gold bows and handed them to Laurel and Brett. Next came a giant teddy bear with a red satin ribbon tied around its neck. "This is for Noelle, as well as something else that is very, very special."

Henry emptied a small, purple velvet drawstring pouch into his palm. "These are yours, Noelle, when you're old enough to know not to swallow them."

Laurel tried to see what he held in his hand, but couldn't.

Brett laughed. "I don't believe it."

Earrings, a ring, some other piece of jewelry? Knowing Henry, it had to be something outrageous. "What is it?" she asked.

"Gold-plated dice," Brett said.

Laurel didn't get it. "Dice?"

"Not just any dice," Henry declared. "One day, my princess, when you're old enough to understand, Uncle Henry will explain how a roll of these dice brought your parents together."

* * * * *

You're not going to believe this offer!

In October and November 2000, buy any two Harlequin or Silhouette books and save $10.00 off future purchases, or buy any three and save $20.00 off future purchases!

Just fill out this form and attach 2 proofs of purchase (cash register receipts) from October and November 2000 books and Harlequin will send you a coupon booklet worth a total savings of $10.00 off future purchases of Harlequin and Silhouette books in 2001. Send us 3 proofs of purchase and we will send you a coupon booklet worth a total savings of $20.00 off future purchases.

Saving money has never been this easy.

I accept your offer! Please send me a coupon booklet:

Name: _____

Address: _____ City: _____

State/Prov.: _____ Zip/Postal Code: _____

Optional Survey!

In a typical month, how many Harlequin or Silhouette books would you buy <u>new</u> at retail stores?

☐ Less than 1 ☐ 1 ☐ 2 ☐ 3 to 4 ☐ 5+

Which of the following statements best describes how you <u>buy</u> Harlequin or Silhouette books? Choose one answer only that <u>best</u> describes you.

☐ I am a regular buyer and reader
☐ I am a regular reader but buy only occasionally
☐ I only buy and read for specific times of the year, e.g. vacations
☐ I subscribe through Reader Service but also buy at retail stores
☐ I mainly borrow and buy only occasionally
☐ I am an occasional buyer and reader

Which of the following statements best describes how you <u>choose</u> the Harlequin and Silhouette series books you buy <u>new</u> at retail stores? By "series," we mean books within a particular line, such as *Harlequin PRESENTS* or *Silhouette SPECIAL EDITION*. Choose one answer only that <u>best</u> describes you.

☐ I only buy books from my favorite series
☐ I generally buy books from my favorite series but also buy books from other series on occasion
☐ I buy some books from my favorite series but also buy from many other series regularly
☐ I buy all types of books depending on my mood and what I find interesting and have no favorite series

Please send this form, along with your cash register receipts as proofs of purchase, to:
In the U.S.: Harlequin Books, P.O. Box 9057, Buffalo, NY 14269
In Canada: Harlequin Books, P.O. Box 622, Fort Erie, Ontario L2A 5X3
(Allow 4-6 weeks for delivery) Offer expires December 31, 2000. PHQ4002

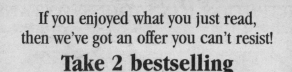

If you enjoyed what you just read,
then we've got an offer you can't resist!

Take 2 bestselling love stories FREE!

Plus get a FREE surprise gift!

Clip this page and mail it to Silhouette Reader Service™

IN U.S.A.	IN CANADA
3010 Walden Ave.	P.O. Box 609
P.O. Box 1867	Fort Erie, Ontario
Buffalo, N.Y. 14240 1867	L2A 5X3

YES! Please send me 2 free Silhouette Romance® novels and my free surprise gift. Then send me 6 brand-new novels every month, which I will receive months before they're available in stores. In the U.S.A., bill me at the bargain price of $2.90 plus 25¢ delivery per book and applicable sales tax, if any*. In Canada, bill me at the bargain price of $3.25 plus 25¢ delivery per book and applicable taxes**. That's the complete price and a savings of at least 10% off the cover prices—what a great deal! I understand that accepting the 2 free books and gift places me under no obligation ever to buy any books. I can always return a shipment and cancel at any time. Even if I never buy another book from Silhouette, the 2 free books and gift are mine to keep forever. So why not take us up on our invitation. You'll be glad you did!

215 SEN C24Q
315 SEN C24R

Name	(PLEASE PRINT)	
Address	Apt.#	
City	State/Prov.	Zip/Postal Code

* Terms and prices subject to change without notice. Sales tax applicable in N.Y.
** Canadian residents will be charged applicable provincial taxes and GST.
All orders subject to approval. Offer limited to one per household.
® are registered trademarks of Harlequin Enterprises Limited.

SROM00_R   ©1998 Harlequin Enterprises Limited